I0621755

Professor Ione D. and the Epicurean Incident

A Steampunk Adventure
Vaughn Treude & Arlys-Allegra Holloway
Nakota Publishing © MMXVII

Professor Ione D. and the Epicurean Incident
Copyright 2017 by Vaughn Treude & Arlys-Allegra Holloway
http://vaughntreude.com

Cover Photos by Arlys-Allegra Holloway
Cover Design by Vaughn Treude
Chapter Illustrations by Kyle Dunbar, Jose Cardenas, Suzanne Stewart
and Kelly Morford.

ISBN: 978-0-9882442-8-3 (Print Edition)

Published by Nakota Publishing
http://nakotapublishing.com

Dedication

I dedicate this book to my children, Arlys Angelique and David Jeffrey, who taught me that humor could be found in almost any situation, and that life is an adventure if you make it so.

Love always,
Arlys-Allegra Holloway

Acknowledgments

We would like to thank the following people and organizations:

Our talented artists, as noted on each illustration.

Lyn Tuchalski for her swift and insightful editing.

Our friends and fellow writers of Nexus, for their critiques, feedback and motivation.

Rissa Watkins, for invaluable input on character and dialog, and beta-reading.

David Nelson, for his ability to detect plot holes and analyze technology

Ron Friedman, for his patient instruction in the merits of pacing and brevity.

John Blohm, for founding the group and motivating us with diverse projects. Many of our writing projects are due to his inspiration.

Our cover models:

Arlys Angelique Endres as Professor Ione Dfrdwy.

Brittney Reed as Emma Farrington.

Anna Nguyen as Lily Chen.

Additional models for chapter illustrations:

David Endres and Cassondra Boyce

Free open-source software used in the production of this book:

Ubuntu Linux operating system, ubuntu.com

Libre Office, a free office productivity suite, libreoffice.org

Calibre, e-book software by Kovid Goyal, calibre-ebook.com

**Chef MacTavish's amazing Culinator Mark II "Angus"
Illustration by Kyle Dunbar**

Table of Contents

Chapter 1. The Epicurean Exhibition   11

Chapter 2. A Dogged Dispute   23

Chapter 3. A Singular Surprise   35

Chapter 4. A Rancorous Rivalry   51

Chapter 5. An Expedient Escort   65

Chapter 6. An Acclaimed Address   77

Chapter 7. The Competition Commence   91

Chapter 8. A Curious Coincidence   105

Chapter 9. A Mysterious Mishap   119

Chapter 10. The Contest Continues   133

Chapter 11. The Four Finalists   144

Chapter 12. MacTavish's Mess   157

Chapter 13. An Impromptu Investigation   171

Chapter 14. A Chase in Cabs   187

Chapter 15. Dangerous Doings   201

Chapter 16. A Culprit Captured   217

Chapter 17. Epicurean Epilogue   231

About the Authors   243

Preview: Prof. Ione D.
            & the Steam-Powered Minotaur   245

Also from Nakota Publishing   261

We arrive at the Crystal Palace for the Royal Epicurean Exhibition.
Illustration by José Cardeñas

London, England, 1901

Chapter 1. The Epicurean Exhibition

"There it is, up ahead, my good lady and gent!" proclaimed the driver in his charming Cockney accent. "The Crystal Palace!"

"Good gracious, it's monstrous," said O'Malley, my traveling companion.

"Monstrous? I find it beautiful." I put my notes aside, then leaned my head out the window of the horse-drawn taxi for a better look. For a moment, I thought the breeze might take my hat, but the weight of the apparatus concealed under the brim held it firmly on my head. I smiled in satisfaction as I withdrew into the passenger compartment. "Just look at it! Do you see how the sun shines on the glass?"

"I didn't mean to imply it was grotesque," my friend explained. "Rather, I didn't expect it to be so huge. Of course, to you, the world traveler, such wonders probably seem rather mundane."

"Not at all." I had to laugh at O'Malley's child-like jealousy. His new position at the *New York Sun* had afforded him little opportunity for travel. This was his first journey abroad in their employ. He had once been a war correspondent for the *Washington Post*, but the end of hostilities in Cuba had meant his reassignment to a tedious position as a copy editor. The *Sun* had rescued him from this purgatory by hiring him to write for their culinary section. Despite the fact that I had earlier applied for this same position, for which I felt I was better qualified than he, I bore him no ill will. We were, after all, long-time friends.

"What I meant was," O'Malley explained, "It's the first time 'cross the Atlantic for me. You, on the other hand, grew up here. So as I said, it would be old hat for you."

"I was only in England between the ages of ten and nineteen," I said. "Still, it's wonderful to be back in London. The air is so much clearer now since they've made the switch from coal to natural gas, so I shan't have the ghastly cough I had at the time. As for the Crystal Palace, I haven't seen it in many years, since my parents last brought me here as a child."

"I should have guessed you'd been here before," grinned O'Malley. "You were off seeing the world when I was sitting in a classroom, memorizing the Presidents of the United States, with my knuckles sore from Sister Agnes rapping them with a ruler."

"Well, since you're a few years older than me, I guess that means you were still making mischief in the upper grades."

"Who, me?" O'Malley laughed. "Perish the thought!"

O'Malley and I had both come from New York, though by separate conveyances, for the First Royal Epicurean Exhibition. Since his costs were covered by his employer, he had taken the luxurious – and expensive – trans-Atlantic Zeppelin *Lord Nelson*. Though I was an invited guest at the event, I still had to pay for my own passage and had taken a much longer journey by ship. My position at Margaret Gallard College in Brooklyn was rewarding in many ways, but not in the financial sense.

The Exhibition, a festival of food and cooking, had been decreed by the recently crowned King Edward, to promote the growth of the restaurant industry and to bolster the reputation of English cuisine. This last item was of particular interest to me. My fascination with the nation and its food had led me to write a history of British cooking, purely for the love of the subject.

"Blimey, look at the queue!" our driver exclaimed. The horse whinnied as we pulled up behind a rattling steam car. "Easy, old fellow! Everybody and his little brother must be here today." He turned his head back to address us. "Apologies, sir and madam, it may be a bit of a wait 'til you can disembark."

"It's quite alright, sir," I said. "Who can be in a hurry on such a lovely day?"

I took the opportunity to quickly review my notes one more time. Though it was a sunny day in London, the interior of the carriage was in deep shadow, making reading difficult. Luckily, I was well prepared. I reached under the brim of my hat and folded down a magnifying lens, which was surrounded by a glowing frame of tubular glass.

"My word, what is that?" asked my traveling companion. "Another of your father's inventions?"

"Yes," I replied, "Though I've made some adaptations and refinements of my own."

"How does it provide illumination, without any heat or flame?"

"Father found a way to synthesize the chemical from the posterior of a lightning bug. All it requires is periodic exposure to sunlight."

"How ingenious!"

"Thank you." I turned to my notes and commenced reading them over for the hundredth time. I was rather nervous about the upcoming event. I had been invited because of the popularity of my book, *The History of British Cooking*. In fact, I was to deliver the keynote address at the opening banquet. Not that I was averse to public speaking, but I would be addressing an assembly of the most honored and accomplished people in the culinary world.

"I was thinking back to when we first met," O'Malley said, startling me from my studies. "You're wearing the exact same hairstyle you were on that day. I recall that I made a remark about it, and you said something about it being Mayan. To this day, I find it quite fetching."

"Thank you," I said, not looking up from my papers. "Someday I shall teach you to duplicate it. Though I suppose your hair is not quite long enough for the braid."

"Then I shall stop getting haircuts," he laughed. "Though I'm not sure how it would go with the color of my hair. I expect it'd make me look like a wild Druidic chieftain."

"Indeed, you would be quite formidable, especially if you grew a beard to match." Though O'Malley found his vivid red hair embarrassing, I thought it was adorable.

I found it sweet that O'Malley had remembered, as I forgotten all about it myself. Then again, his sharp memory and keen eye for detail had helped make him a successful journalist at the age of twenty-six.

I thought back to the day when my family had arrived in Washington, D.C., after spending a year in Guatemala. As it was several weeks before I could resume my studies, I occupied much of my time that summer at the Smithsonian Institution. Thomas O'Malley was then a tour guide at the Museum of Natural History. We became fast friends, and he was a regular visitor to my family's home in Georgetown.

"Are you still going over your speech?" O'Malley asked.

"I just want to make a good impression. This being a Royal Exhibition and all, one never knows who will be in attendance."

"Oh, you're not nervous, are you, Professor D?" O'Malley said with a grin. "I should think by this time you could deliver your speech backwards if you had a mind to. Don't worry, though, I'm sure the King will be quite impressed. If nothing else, he'll love your hair."

"That's good to hear," I said, returning to my notes, mouthing the words silently in an attempt to etch them in my memory.

Fate, however, was determined not to allow me to concentrate. The carriage, which had been creeping forward, jerked to a halt. From outside came the sound of voices shouting. They were chanting in unison, "Home Rule for Ireland!"

"What's going on?" asked O'Malley. "I didn't expect there would be any altercations."

"Bloody Irish!" the cabbie grumbled. "I'd steer clear of those troublemakers if I was you. Hopefully, the constabulary will clear them out soon."

"They are citizens of the United Kingdom," said O'Malley. "Don't they deserve a chance to air their grievances?"

"If it were up to me," the driver said. "I'd ship the lot of them troublemakers back to their potato fields."

My friend opened his mouth as if to retort, but then closed it and shook his head.

I glanced through the open window at our driver, surprised at his comment. Though O'Malley didn't speak with any sort of brogue, I'd have thought his red hair and freckles would have been a dead giveaway.

Ever the reporter, O'Malley opened his satchel and retrieved his notebook. He stared out the window at the protesters with their hand-painted signs, diligently making notes in pencil. I found myself captivated by the intensity of his gaze. I had forgotten how blue his eyes were. As he began writing on a new page, the lead broke, and he looked away from the window.

At that moment, our eyes met. He gave me an enigmatic smile before digging out another pencil and resuming his writing. I returned to my work as well, feeling a warmth in my cheeks. I hoped I was not blushing.

It had been at least two years since I had last seen O'Malley, though we had corresponded the entire time. The memory of our courtship brought a touch of melancholy to my mood. At the time, I was certain he was about to propose marriage. Indeed, he spent several hours on the porch with my father one evening, sharing brandy and a conversation to which I was not privy. As I helped my mother clean up the supper dishes, she was all smiles, making remarks such as "Your father and I were wed in June, but I think the autumn is also a very romantic season, no?"

My friend said nothing about their discussion, nor would Father answer my questions about it. The very next day, however, Thomas came to me with unexpected news. "I've been promoted to a full-time reporter!"

"How wonderful!" I cried. "I suppose you shall be obliged to give up your part-time work at the Smithsonian."

"Of course. And that's not all! They're sending me to Havana, to report on the troubles down in Cuba. Some say America may even become involved in the war!"

"That is a splendid opportunity! I wish I could go as well; it sounds very exciting." Despite the smile on my face, there was a pang of sadness in my heart.

For a moment he was silent, making me wonder if he had discerned my thoughts. He sighed and said, "You and I both know that this is a very dangerous assignment, and is no place for a woman."

"Mr. O'Malley, I'll have you know." I wagged my finger at him, continuing, "I can shoot a gun, I can ride a horse, I can protect myself as well as any man. In fact..."

"Ione, please," Tom interrupted. "I couldn't bear the thought of anything happening to you. And I will miss you terribly."

"I'll miss you, too. But please, please be careful."

He laughed. "If I can survive being the youngest of twelve brothers and sisters, I can survive anything!"

Thomas never did propose to me, which was a disappointment but also a relief, because I was not sure what my answer would have been. Though he was very dear to me, and I was in no way opposed to marriage, I simply was not ready. I had one more year of college to finish my degree, after which I had hoped to travel and see the world, with no husband to tell me which places were "too dangerous for a woman."

"Well here we are, at last!" the driver exclaimed, bringing me back to the present as the carriage halted once again. O'Malley sprang from his seat and bounded out of the door, where he stood, holding it open for me.

I hurried to put away my notes. When I reached under the seat for my handbag, my hat, weighed down by the light-and-magnifier apparatus, slipped off my head and slid under the bench across from me. I was forced to bend down low to retrieve it as O'Malley waited, an amused smile on his face.

In the meantime, our driver had gone around back to retrieve my valise from the back of the carriage and stood next to O'Malley waiting for his payment. Over the chanting of the men and ladies on the nearby walkway, I heard him muttering, "Dad-blasted Irish." He turned to my friend and said, "That'll be two shillings, please."

O'Malley paid him. I noticed that, despite my friend's obvious disgust with the man's remarks, he threw in a few pence as a tip.

I hastened to disembark while O'Malley was thus occupied, but I was too late. He was back at the carriage door in a flash. He took a hold of my hand to help me step down.

In my frustration, I stopped and said, "That's so very kind of you, Thomas, but I am quite capable."

"After all this time, Ione. Please, call me Tom."

"Yes, O'Malley," I replied with a smile. "I don't know why you men persist in thinking we women are fragile. After all, I climbed the temple pyramids..." As I said those words, my foot slipped on the step of the carriage and I fell forward toward him. He put both his hands on my arms to catch me; his grip was firm and yet gentle. Somehow my face stopped inches from his.

We stood there for a long moment, staring into each other's eyes. It was if we had never been separated. Then, just as I thought he might be about to act on some wild impulse to kiss me, there came the sound of shouting.

"Watch out! Runaway car!"

With his strong arms, O'Malley thrust me back into the carriage. My handbag flew from my grasp and I landed on my back on the floor of the compartment. The vehicle shook as the horse reared and whinnied. "Bloody hell!" cried the cabbie.

All I could see was a crowd of frantic people rushing by. My friend was nowhere to be seen.

"O'Malley!" I cried. "Tom, are you alright?"

Heroic Tom saves a little boy from a runaway motorcar.
Illustration by José Cardeñas

Chapter 2. A Dogged Dispute

I could scarcely breathe as I struggled to my feet and stepped out of the carriage. My eyes darted over the scene of mayhem. Where was Tom, I wondered as I rushed past the flustered cabbie through the agitated crowd. A car lay on its side, wheels spinning, its boiler spewing steam.

"Help! Doctor!" someone shouted. Somewhere a child was shrieking. At least three people lay sprawled on the brick walkway. My heart stopped for a moment as I spied a familiar pair of ugly leather boots amongst them. The boots moved, and O'Malley rose from the ground, dusting himself off. I gave a silent prayer of thanks.

"Tom!" I cried as I made my way through the crowd, but he turned away and knelt down.

"There, there, young fellow," he said. "You're just scraped up a bit, you'll be fine."

A frantic woman rushed up and scooped the crying little boy into her arms. "Oh thank you, sir, you have saved my Horace's life!"

O'Malley stood again and smiled. "I was just in the right place at the right time. Saints be praised that the boy wasn't harmed!"

"Thank goodness you're safe!" I cried, rushing up to hug Tom. I glanced toward the child, who was now in his mother's arms, and had stopped crying.

"I shall have to keep a closer eye on you from now on," the mother said.

"You as well," I said to Tom, releasing him from my impulsive embrace.

"That steam car almost ran the boy over," he explained, scanning the crowd. "No one was driving; it went out of control somehow. I wonder where the owner is."

"Thomas – Tom – I was quite worried about you," I said.

He looked at me and laughed. "I should think a, 'thank you for saving my life' should suffice."

"Of course, thank you, Tom! You've saved two lives today. Perhaps you shall be in the news, rather than reporting it."

"I should hope not," he said. "Madam," he turned to speak to the child's mother, but she had already disappeared into the throng. "If only I could find a witness who might answer a few questions."

"I see the police have arrived," I said. "They will probably have some questions of their own for the hero of the day."

O'Malley sighed. "We have already missed the opening ceremonies. I hate to be a bad citizen, but if I'm detained for a police interview, we shall be even later. I suggest we hurry along to the exhibition hall."

"Agreed," I said, offering him my arm.

As O'Malley had noted, we had missed the exhibition's opening, which had been attended by King Edward himself. We were not the only tardy ones. The line of people waiting to enter the Crystal Palace stretched well past where we had disembarked, and we were obliged to walk some distance further to reach its end.

"I guess we shall have a wait a while more," Tom said as we joined the queue.

"It's not so bad," I said. "Look how well-dressed everyone is! I simply love seeing all the latest fashions and finery."

He shrugged. "I suppose. I'm no fashion reporter, though."

"No, you're not," I laughed. "I noticed you're still wearing those dreadful old boots."

"I bought them in Cuba," he said. "They're quite comfortable, and I have a sentimental attachment to them."

"Hopefully no one will look at your feet," I said.

Excluding his footwear, O'Malley looked quite handsome in his workaday brown suit. It was, I assumed, the best he could afford on his reporter's salary. Still, he wore it with pride, his matching bowler hat tipped at a jaunty angle. He had the air of a man who was going places in the world.

I myself wore my best summer outfit; a long peach-colored dress with frilly sleeves complemented an ivory white lace jacket. I wore my dark hair up, fastened in Mayan-style braids and topped with the modified hat I described earlier. On my feet were my favorite ostrich leather riding boots. Few people would guess these were actually men's boots I had acquired in Argentina and altered to fit. My prized possession, however, was my handbag, made of imported teak wood with brass handles. My father had helped me to construct it to my own specifications.

"Being here again brings back fond memories," I said. "My mother would sometimes bring me here shopping on Saturdays."

"Shopping?" O'Malley replied. "I didn't realize they had shops here." He looked around as we inched forward. "Windmills!" he exclaimed. "Were these present when you were a child?"

"No. I heard they were built to provide the Palace with electrical power. I imagine it looks most impressive in the evening, all lit up from within."

"Speaking of impressive," O'Malley pointed to a lake that dominated the Palace grounds. "Look, the dinosaurs!" In and around the lake stood more than a dozen large concrete statues of prehistoric creatures.

"They seemed so huge and terrifying when I was a child," I said. "The gift shop sold miniatures of them, which I found far more interesting than the china dolls I had previously collected. My father indulged me by buying me a model of the iguanodon."

"You probably displayed it as the centerpiece of your room."

"Of course," I replied. "Much to my mother's chagrin."

"Please stay close, Ione," O'Malley said as we waited. "Remember what our driver said about those rabble-rousers."

"You need not worry," I said, "I have studied several defensive techniques. If the need arises, I would not hesitate to protect you."

O'Malley laughed out loud. "My dear, you have the most splendid sense of humor."

I smiled sweetly in response, though what I'd told him was true. Starting at the age of six, Father arranged for me to train in several Oriental fighting arts, which Mother grudgingly accepted. When I studied judo, she made my uniform by hand. It was fencing, however, that I enjoyed the most, which is why I always carried an extra-long hat pin.

27

It was that moment that one of those so-called rabble-rousers appeared. "Excuse me, sir, miss," said a woman's voice with a melodic lilt. She wore a modest working-class skirt and blouse. "We'd like you to have some information about the plight of the Irish." She thrust a pamphlet into my hand.

'Home Rule for Ireland,' read the headline. 'It's Only Fair!'

"I certainly do sympathize," I told her. "Though I am not a British subject."

"What about you, sir?" she asked O'Malley "If ye don't mind me sayin', you've got the look of the Emerald Isle about ye."

"That's correct," he replied with a smile. "My mother and father hail from County Cork. And what part of Ireland are you from?"

"Alright, that's enough," interrupted a booming male voice. A man in a London police uniform appeared beside the Irish woman. "Proselytizing for any cause is prohibited in this park. Kindly move along or I'll place you under arrest."

The woman's mouth fell open in shock. "Why I never! I'm a married lady and a good Catholic."

"I'm not talking about that, you stupid woman," snapped the officer. "Leave now or you'll join the others in the paddy wagon." He gestured down the road, where his fellow police were shepherding a number of handcuffed protesters into the back of a horse-drawn wagon.

"Very well," the woman replied with a scowl. "But remember what the Good Book says, 'whatsoever ye sow, that ye shall also reap.'"

"I said now," the policeman snapped as he escorted the incensed woman away.

"What's that smile about?" O'Malley asked me. "Surely you don't find the officer's rudeness amusing."

"Oh, no," I chuckled. "I was just thinking about how desperate the poor woman must be, to resort to proselytizing."

O'Malley shook his head. "Someday, Ione, your lack of decorum will get you in trouble."

"Why Tom, I was simply talking about pamphleting," I teased. "I do feel bad about the protesters being arrested. Though I imagine the authorities are worried about possible violence."

O'Malley scowled. "If the British don't allow for peaceful change, it will be like 1776 all over again."

"You may be right," I agreed.

As we arrived at the entrance we handed our tickets to a pair of handsome young doormen. Though they wore tuxedos, each of them had a glint of brass protruding from his right sleeve. I recognized them as weapons gauntlets, revealing that the doormen also functioned as guards.

I had seen soldiers wearing similar devices on my family's trip to Vienna. With their ornate scroll-work and intricate enameled designs, they combined beauty with deadliness. Most contained a blade, a small pistol or both. Alas, my parents forbade me to purchase one, declaring them not fitting for a young lady to possess. However, my father did give me a book about them.

Just as we were entering, one of the guards took notice of my unusual purse. "May I examine your um... handbag, miss?"

I clenched my teeth in a forced smile. "Am I allowed to decline?"

"No miss; not if you want to be admitted."

I sighed and handed him the purse. I took pleasure in his inability to open it; I was obliged to show him the recessed latch. Embarrassed, the man peered inside briefly, then handed it back to me. "Thank you, miss."

I nodded and rejoined O'Malley who had been waiting patiently just inside the entry way.

"I noticed they didn't search you, Tom. I certainly wouldn't trust you. You could hide any number of knives or small pistols in the inside pockets of your coat."

"Don't give them any ideas," O'Malley laughed. "As much as I admire the creativity of your accessories," he said, looking at my bag, "I doubt it would have attracted as much attention had it looked like a normal purse."

"I would be glad to carry a normal purse," I replied, "If I were able to find one that was both elegant and practical."

As we proceeded into the great hall, the delightful smells hit us. Though we had enjoyed a dinner of ham and potatoes on the train into London, the overpowering presence of fine cooking was enough to stimulate my appetite. Booths and stalls exhibiting foods of all kinds lined the broad entry hall.

"This is all quite fascinating," I said. "I doubt one could see everything the Exhibition has to offer in the short time allotted to it." Hearing no response, I looked around for my companion. "Tom?"

I found him at a nearby vendor's table, where he was about to purchase a giant turkey leg.

"Tom, shouldn't we proceed to the registration table first?"

"Eh? Yes, I suppose I should go get my press credentials. And I imagine the management will want to know their keynote speaker has arrived." He reached into his pocket for a piece of paper, which he unfolded and studied.

"Perhaps we want to go in that direction." I pointed to a sign that said 'REGISTRATION' with an arrow pointing to the left.

O'Malley gave me a sniff of disdain. We headed in the direction of the arrow. We had not gone far when we came to an area enclosed with whitewashed clapboard walls. In the midst of the partition was a door with a frosted glass window on top. The painted legend said 'Management Office.' Beneath was a hand-lettered sign that said 'GUEST REGISTRATION.'

We proceeded inside, where we encountered a dour looking woman in a conservative gray dress sitting behind a desk. She searched through a ledger to find our names, then handed us each an ornate badge with a ribbon. O'Malley's badge had the word 'REPORTER' stamped upon it and a red ribbon. Mine was embossed with the words 'SPECIAL GUEST,' and the attached ribbon was gold. "Once again, I out-rank you," I said to my companion. He just shook his head and sighed.

After leaving the office, we proceeded to the building's main concourse, which featured even more exhibits. All appeared to be food-related. Some displayed cooking techniques, some sold food, and others dispensed wines and beer.

"It's difficult to decide where to go first," I said.

"Suddenly I'm quite thirsty," O'Malley said, looking longingly toward the nearest beer vendor.

"Ione!" called a woman's voice. "I was beginning to think I'd never find you!"

Emma, my best friend from school, surprises me by
showing up at the Exhibition.
Illustration by Suzanne Stewart.

Chapter 3. A Singular Surprise

I whirled around to see who had spoken. When I realized who it was, my mouth fell open in surprise. "Emma! I didn't know you were going to be here!"

She rushed over to embrace me. "I would have written you, but it was a last-minute opportunity." Stepping back to look at me, she added, "You look stunning!"

"As do you. No one would guess you're the mother of two," I said.

Emma had been my best friend at Lady Worcester's School for Girls. She seemed scarcely changed, but for the new style of clothing. Her auburn hair was tied back with an ivory clasp into a single strand that cascaded down her shoulders. She wore a deep green dress with silvery highlights. What stood out, however, was her hat. A broad-brimmed white straw hat with a matching ribbon, adorned with black feathers and a bow, framed her perfect face. I couldn't help but notice an over-sized hat pin.

"You wore your charm bracelet," Emma said. "Mine never leaves my wrist."

I held it up and jingled it. "Is that a pyramid?" she asked. "How adorable!"

"Thank you," I said. "It's such a delightful surprise to see you!"

"How could I stay away, with you being the keynote speaker and all?" She looked over at Tom. "Are you going to introduce me to your handsome companion?"

"Oh, I'm sorry. Emma, this is Thomas O'Malley. He's a reporter for the *New York Post* and rescuer of small children."

Emma gasped. "Are you the hero who saved that little boy from certain death by that runaway car?"

"And me, too," I added.

"Goodness, you're a double hero!"

Tom smiled, his fair face reddening. "I happened to be there at the time. I'm just glad that no one was hurt in the mishap." He gave a brief bow. "So Ione, who is your charming friend?"

"Tom, this is my dear friend Emma Giles-Whitley."

My friend's smile disappeared as she eyed me sternly.

"Oops, pardon me. It's Mrs. Nigel Farrington now. Emma and I attended school together."

"Yes," Emma laughed. "We were called the Fabulous Four. Ione and myself, of course, and Cynthia and Margery." She studied Tom again. "O'Malley, I've heard that name. You're the rogue who abandoned Ione to traipse around the swamps in Santo Domingo?"

"Actually, it was Cuba. I was assigned to cover the Spanish-American War. It was hot, humid, and unpleasant but thankfully the war was a short one."

"Oh, how interesting." Emma turned back to me. "Ione, we have so much catching up to do! I hope you won't be too busy for me."

"Tom and I were going to walk down the promenade and take in the exhibits. I insist that you join us, of course."

"Of course," Emma said.

Tom cleared his throat. "You ladies will have to excuse me. I promised I would send my supervisor a telegram the moment I arrived at the Exhibition."

"We will excuse you-- this time," Emma said with a smile.

"It was a pleasure meeting you, Mrs. Farrington. Ione, I will see you at the banquet." He tipped his hat and departed.

"It's so exciting!" Emma took my arm in hers as we started along the broad promenade that ran down the length of the great structure. "My dear Ione, a best-selling author. I've brought my copy of your book, which I insist you sign for me."

"Of course," I said. "How are the children? And Nigel? Did they come with you?"

"Nigel is on a hunting trip with the mayor of Luton and the Archdeacon of Chesterfield."

"Goodness, dear Nigel is really moving up in the world. And the children?"

"They're with Nigel's mother at Chatterley Hall. I found myself footloose and fancy-free, so I hopped on the train to London."

"I'm so glad you did. I've really missed you. Have you gotten a chance to look around?"

"Not really. I arrived here about an hour ago and I've spent all that time looking for you. I haven't even checked into a hotel yet. Where are you staying?"

"I have reservations at the Harrogate. We sent the taxi driver to deliver my bags, but I haven't yet been there."

"Marvelous! That's a fine establishment. I shall stay there as well."

"Brilliant," I replied. "Hmm, what shall we see first?"

"The food smells wonderful," she said, as we walked through the vendor area. "Though I had dinner on the train."

"At the moment I'm too excited to eat. We can return to this area later."

"Agreed," Emma said. "Look, over there, isn't that amazing?"

I turned my head to follow her line of sight. Down the walkway ahead of us, just beyond the food sellers, I saw the gleam of brass and chrome. Stretching before us were countless booths and exhibits featuring the latest innovations in kitchen gadgetry. These were the labor-saving devices that would bring gourmet cooking to every home. Scores of customers milled about, as the sellers demonstrated their wares. The sounds of motors and gears were audible over the hubbub of the crowd.

"Yes," I breathed, transfixed. "What an incredible array of culinary inventions."

Emma laughed. "I was referring to that young lady's ostrich-plume hat. As for the kitchen gadgets, I can't say I know much about that sort of thing. You know me; I can scarcely boil water without burning it. As far as I'm concerned, the best labor saving device one can acquire is a good cook!"

"Oh, Emma." I laughed at the unconscious admission of her privileged station in life. "Then what shall it be?" We stopped in front of a directory map of the Exhibition. "Besides the kitchen devices, there are the food sellers, the grocery wholesalers, and agricultural exhibits."

"You mean chickens, pigs and such? The smell must be dreadful. Let's stay on this side, shall we?"

"Agreed. But I do want to see some of those inventions. My students will be fascinated to hear about them."

"That will be fine," my friend said. "As long as we get to spend some time together. So Ione, what's it like to be a professor?"

"It's wonderful. Teaching is a rewarding profession, and I have time to pursue my own research."

"I don't mean the job so much as the prestige. It's a real honor isn't it?"

"I don't feel any different, if that's what you mean. But I'd like to hear about you. Is it exciting to be married to a Member of Parliament?"

Emma shrugged. "Yes and no. Political matters are dreadfully dull, but I've met some very interesting people. For example, have you met Dame Leonora from the Epicurean Society? What a delightful woman! She knows everyone who is anyone in the culinary world."

"I hear she's in charge of the cooking contest here at the Exhibition," I said. "I'm quite looking forward to meeting her. Perhaps you can introduce me."

"I doubt that will be necessary. Surely she'll be sitting with you at the head table at tonight's banquet. By the way, will Mr. O'Malley be your escort? I imagine they'll be expecting you to sit with a companion."

"I hadn't thought about it," I said. "Couldn't you be my escort instead?"

"Goodness, you are as silly as you always were," she giggled. "So do I gather that you and Mr. O'Malley are not..."

"As I have told you repeatedly in my letters," I said, smiling despite my annoyance. "Tom and I are good friends, nothing more."

"That's too bad," she said. "I believe you mentioned that he loves travel and adventure, just like you do. You could accompany him to exotic places and do research for your next book!"

"Emma, you have a very romantic view of things. Tom is a journalist and has his own work that occupies his time." Hoping to deflect her attempts at match-making, I lead her toward the exhibits. "Look at that fascinating device!"

One of the exhibitors, a tall slender man with unruly gray hair, and a gray-streaked beard and goatee, stepped out to greet us. "Good afternoon, ladies. Allow me to show you my latest creation."

"Good afternoon, sir," I replied. "My friend and I were just browsing."

"It will take but a moment," the man said. He spoke English well but sounded neither like an Englishman nor an American.

"Behold the Potatomatic, my personal design. Insert the potatoes, one at a time, into this opening here." He pulled back a hinged lid covering a chrome-plated pipe, then dropped the vegetable inside. "Then pull this lever." A tiny steam engine came to life. Through a glass window in the machine, we could see the potato proceeding down a conveyor where it was scrubbed, peeled, and then diced into small cubes.

"My," I admitted, "It certainly is an impressive contraption. It would work well for the dining hall at the college where I work, but how practical would it be for an individual home?"

"On the contrary, this device is very useful and so easy to learn that even the simplest of hired help can operate it."

"I don't doubt that," I admitted, "But its size alone makes it impractical for the typical family. And I can imagine it takes considerable effort to clean."

At this, the man scowled and exhaled loudly. "If you cannot appreciate the brilliance of this machine, kindly move along. This device will soon be in every home."

"I for one would not buy it," Emma interjected. "My family doesn't eat nearly enough potatoes to justify the cost. It's too loud and it smells of kerosene. Besides, everybody knows that electricity is the wave of the future."

"That's preposterous!" The man shouted. In his agitation, his foreign accent became more pronounced. "Everyone knows that electricity is dangerous. If you wish to blow yourself up, fine. That would be one less ignorant person in the world."

"You will never sell your product with hostility and condescension," I said. "Much less put one in every kitchen."

The man stepped out from behind the counter and approached us, his face reddening with anger. "Do you presume to tell me how to run my business?"

I glanced at Emma, who had moved her hand toward the long pin concealed in her hat.

"I wouldn't dream of it," I grabbed my friend's arm and led her away. I glanced back to see that the man standing at his booth, glaring at us.

As we continued down the concourse, Emma lowered her voice and said, "Can you believe that man?"

I shook my head. "His behavior was appalling. Why would he become so agitated about a potato chopper?"

"He plainly knows nothing about women," Emma added.

"But that's not the only thing that bothers me. I couldn't quite place his accent. It became more pronounced when he got angry. And did you notice he had nothing but the demonstration model? Where was his inventory for sale?"

"Maybe he's just a bad businessman," Emma suggested. "Though for a moment, I thought he might physically assault you."

"The situation did get a bit tense. Then I saw your hand go up to your hat pin. You were ready to defend me!" I said with a grin.

"You know how the song goes – 'Never go out without your hat pin,'" Emma giggled. "Let's speak of something more pleasant. Are you still corresponding with that dashing young Mexican – what was his name?"

"Batista," I said. "And no, we haven't exchanged letters for some time. As I told you, he was involved in some dishonest dealings involving artifacts in Tikal."

"Well, if he and Tom are both out of the running," Emma said, "I can't think of a better place than this to meet an eligible bachelor. I was looking at the program, and some of the officials whom I know just happen to be unmarried."

"Emma, please," I said. "I appreciate your concern, but..."

"Even if you're not ready to buy, the shopping is still enjoyable," she said with a wink.

"Oh, look over there! 'All Things Garlic.' I love cooking with garlic."

"Just like your mother," Emma said.

We approached the vendor's exhibit. Two women sat behind a table upon which all sorts of metal objects had been laid. One of them stood and greeted us, "Buongiorno, signorinas. Are you connoisseurs of garlic? It is the spice that is as healthful as it is flavorful."

She showed us various gadgets designed to chop, dice and puree garlic. I purchased a mincer, which was small enough to fit in my purse.

Emma turned to me and said, "With all these wonderful smells, I'm suddenly famished. Now would be a great time to have a taste of the exquisite food that's all around us."

"Agreed. I'm quite anxious to try some of these new and unique dishes." We strolled down the promenade of the Palace, toward a sign labeled 'Hall of Restaurants.'

We had not been the only ones with this idea, as a large crowd was now gathering. Here there were long lines of tables bearing all sorts of food, on both sides of the hallway and also down the middle. People chose plates and cutlery from tables at the entry and placed them on wooden trays. Uniformed servers dished out food at the customers' request. It was a procedure now fashionable in the cafeterias of Paris.

Children and young adults, attired like the servers in white shirts or blouses and black pants or skirts, kept the tables clear of dirty dishes and utensils. Some looked to be less than ten years old. It saddened me to think of such young ones working so hard.

"What on earth is that smell?" Emma sniffed. "I thought the fare was supposed to be British."

I couldn't help but laugh. "Escargot! This is 'International Day,' after all. As I recall, you adored my mother's French cooking."

"French cooking is *tres magnifique*, I agree. As long as one isn't expected to eat snails." She wrinkled her nose in disgust.

"You should try them; you might find you enjoy them."

"Please, Ione, I prefer not to think of them. I've seen the horrible little beasts in my garden. Nigel keeps bringing them inside."

"That sounds troublesome." I nodded. "Look, over there. They have caviar! I don't often get to have that."

"Now there's something we can both agree upon," Emma said.

We took our places at the end of the queue. Though it moved slowly, we had plenty to talk about. As Emma was filling me in about the doings of all our friends from school, a sudden loud sound caused her to whirl around so quickly she almost lost her hat.

"What was that?" she exclaimed.

When I realized what it was, I had to laugh. "Whoever is playing those bagpipes must be rather a novice."

"Yes," laughed Emma. "I thought for a moment a cat had been stepped on. Look at the crowds! I wonder what's happening over there."

I stood on tip-toe in an attempt to see. "Could King Edward have arrived?"

"I wouldn't get my hopes up, dear," Emma said. "His Majesty is much too busy to attend every event he sponsors. Besides, His Royal Highness would be announced by the celestial sound of trumpets, not the barbaric cacophony the highlanders call music."

"Well, in any case," I countered, "I'd like to see what the cause of the commotion is."

"But Ione," Emma complained. "We're almost to the front of the line."

"I'll catch up with you later, then," I said. "I'm not all that fond of caviar anyway. It's too salty for my taste."

"Alright," Emma sighed.

With that, I turned and hastened across the vast promenade. The piping had grown louder, and the sound echoed all around. The throng had grown as well, and I found myself wishing for a chair to stand upon, as I am not particularly tall.

I stepped up next to a flamboyantly dressed couple, she in an orange-colored dress, he in a straw hat and pin-striped suit, standing at the edge of the fracas. "Excuse me," I raised my voice to be heard over the din, "Do you know what the cause of all the excitement is?"

The woman looked at me in surprise. "It's Mad Chef MacTavish, ain't you heard of him?"

"Indeed I have," I said. "His restaurant Ha Senoiad is the premier culinary establishment in Glasgow. I was not aware he was attending this event."

"Attending?" laughed her husband. "He's the bloomin' center of attention."

Professor Ione D. & the Epicurean Incident

Chef "Mad" MacTavish arrives with his amazing
automaton Angus.
Illustration by José Cardeñas

Chapter 4. A Rancorous Rivalry

At that moment a pair of the tuxedo-clad guards we had seen at the door appeared and made their way past us, parting the crowd as they went. "Ladies and gentlemen! Kindly step back and allow Mr. MacTavish to proceed."

The crowd erupted in applause amid scattered shouts of "Charlatan!" and "Blackguard!"

MacTavish was the focus of many stories about his eccentric culinary genius. I simply had to get through the throng so I could see him. "Excuse me, beg your pardon," I said as I worked my way forward.

When I reached the front of the crowd, I immediately recognized MacTavish's face from the many newspaper articles. He had a thick reddish beard and wild curly hair to match, topped by a Scottish tam o'shanter. He wore a long-sleeved white shirt under a vest of red and black tartan, and a kilt to match. In one hand he carried an ornately carved wooden walking stick.

Following behind him was the source of the piping. Though I had expected a Scotsman in similar dress, I was excited to see an automaton with a set of bagpipes fastened via a leather strap about its midsection. On its lower portions, it wore a kilt, a perfect match for MacTavish's. I couldn't help but giggle at the sight.

The automaton stood six feet tall with a skin of gleaming brass and rubber-tyred wheels for locomotion. Its head was a glass bubble with a pair of camera-like lenses, topped with a cap exactly like MacTavish's. Its chest was covered with dials and gauges. On each side of its torso were mounted an articulated mechanical arm. One arm pumped the bagpipe's cow-skin sack to produce the droning harmony, while the other worked the melody pipe to produce an intricate melody. Since the metal man had no mouth, the pipe received air from a black rubber tube plugged into a socket in its abdomen.

The excited chatter of the crowd was audible even over the wailing of the pipes. I heard cries of "Amazing!" and "Astonishing!"

"It's the devil's work!" someone else shouted. "An abomination!"

As I watched, fascinated, the machine came to a halt and ceased playing. The drones stopped in mid-note, trailing off in a squawk.

MacTavish whirled around and brandished his walking stick at the automaton. "Why, ye vile collection of gears and plumbing, I should sell ye for scrap!" A hush came over the crowd, and the chef took a moment to compose himself. "Such malfunctions are quite out of the ordinary," he said. "Old Angus can be a bit finicky at times, but he's the most valuable assistant I've ever had." He put his arm around the machine and patted it on the metal shoulder.

"Maybe that's because that thing don't require any wages," chuckled a man standing beside me.

"A true Scotsman," added his wife, hiding her laughter behind a gloved hand.

Several journalists had made their way to the front of the crowd, though I did not see Tom among them. One man carried one of the new portable box cameras. His assistant, a boy in his mid-teens, held up a pedestal on which he ignited some flash powder for the photograph.

"Mr. MacTavish!" A pretty girl in a frilly pink dress rushed into the clearing around him. "Could you please sign your book for me?" She thrust forward a cookbook.

"Certainly, my dear!" He opened a compartment on the automaton's side, from which he withdrew pen and ink. With a theatrical flourish, he signed the book, then handed it back to her.

"Ooh, thank you, sir!" the girl curtsied to her idol, then disappeared into the crowd.

"He autographs his cookbooks!" I remarked. "What a shame that I didn't bring one."

"Not to worry, I'd wager he carries some spares with him, just in case a pretty girl was to ask. You're just the sort who'd catch his eye," the man standing beside me said with a wink.

I laughed and said, "Is that so?"

"I quite admire the bloke," said his wife. "How he does things his own way and flaunts convention. That's why the papers call him 'Mad.'"

"To break the rules in an effective way, you must first know them well," I replied.

"Quite a clever chap, for a Scotsman," said a voice from behind me.

I smelled a whiff of smoke and turned around. There stood Tom with the fellow whom I had not met. His companion's aristocratic face and athletic physique more than made up for his premature baldness, though there was a hint of arrogance in his expression.

"Ione!" Tom greeted me. "Where is your friend, Mrs. Farrington?"

"She didn't want to leave the caviar line."

"Harrison, I'd like to introduce Professor Ione D. of Margaret Gallard College. She's the head of the culinary department there. Ione, this is Gerald Harrison of the Times of London."

"It's a pleasure to meet you," I said, offering my hand.

Harrison removed the pipe from his mouth and placed it in his jacket pocket. "I'm charmed to meet such an elegant lady from America." He bowed slightly and, instead of shaking my hand, he kissed it. I could feel the bristles of his mustache through my thin linen glove.

"You have a very interesting surname," Harrison said. "Is it perhaps French in origin?"

"It's an initial," I explained. "My family name is Dfrdwy, after the Welsh river of the same name. So many of my classmates found it difficult to pronounce, that one of my instructors took to calling me Miss D. and it's been that ever since."

"Miss Dfrdwy." O'Malley said, pronouncing it perfectly, "Is the youngest woman to achieve a full professorship in the history of Gallard College. She is one of the most intelligent and widely traveled people I know."

I gave him a look. His extravagant compliments could be a bit embarrassing at times.

"Well done, Professor." Harrison turned back to Tom. "Speaking of accomplishments, old chap, now that's impressive. Look at the pretty girls waiting in line for MacTavish's signature."

Presently the chef was ignoring his female admirers as he peered inside the access panel on Angus' back.

"The machine he's tinkering with is his latest invention, the MacTavish Automatic Culinator," I said. "I simply must have a closer look at it."

"I've heard a lot about this MacTavish." O'Malley declared. "I hadn't heard whether he was planning to participate in the Exhibition."

"We must obtain an interview," Harrison said. He pushed his way forward through the crowd, leaving O'Malley and me behind.

"Mr. MacTavish," said Harrison, holding up his notebook. "I represent the Times of London. Do you wish to say something to our readers about the upcoming All-Britain Cooking Competition?"

"Just a wee moment. MacTavish was still bent over Angus, adjusting something with a screwdriver. He jumped back as the automaton came to life with a whirring of gears and a brief squeal from the pipes.

MacTavish straightened up with pride as Harrison waited with his notebook. "Most assuredly I will be participating," he said. "Among the many entrants, not one is my equal. I have already cleared a place in my restaurant's trophy case."

The crowd's reaction was polite applause, with a smattering of cheers and boos.

"A truly humble man," I said to O'Malley with a mischievous grin. "I was skeptical at first, but the warmth of his personality has won me over."

"Oh, Ione," Tom replied, shaking his head.

"Mr. MacTavish," called an unfamiliar voice. "I see you have automated not just your cooking staff, but the entertainment as well. Perhaps this metal garbage can will be replacing you, too, thus sparing your customers much gastronomic distress."

The insult provoked numerous gasps from the onlookers, as well as scattered laughter.

"Why it's Fenimore!" MacTavish stepped forward to shake the newcomer's hand. "I'm pleased to see you here. It gives me yet another chance to best you in culinary skill." This remark brought forth loud cheers from the crowd.

The newcomer was a slight man with thinning gray hair and a thin mustache; he wore a conservative gray suit that matched them perfectly. Though I had never seen him before, I knew who MacTavish was addressing: his arch-nemesis, Sir Charles Fenimore.

"Who is this fellow?" O'Malley whispered to me.

"Charles Fenimore," I explained. "The cooking prodigy of York. At age 15 he won the coveted Cardiff Prize for his Cornish game hen. Later on, his cooking impressed Queen Victoria so much that she knighted him."

"No wonder he looked familiar," O'Malley said. "There was a sketch of him on the front page of the Times."

Fenimore was not alone. At his left stood a woman, perhaps his wife. She was equal in height and much broader; she wore an ivory dress with a now-unfashionable bustle. As the two men continued their verbal sparring match, she gave a loud sigh and turned away.

Following behind the couple was a slight man dressed in traditional Oriental garb: a blue pajama-like suit. His hair was done in the Chinese fashion, shaved in the front and bound in a long pigtail behind. He glared at the Scotsman with particular malice, then moved forward to stand behind Fenimore, his muscles tensed as if readying himself for combat in some Asian fighting discipline.

MacTavish seemed oblivious to the Chinaman's hostility. His eyes were fixed upon his antagonist as if he expected the small man to pounce on him.

"I welcome the opportunity to compete with you," Fenimore said, "Though I shan't be surprised if your entry is disqualified. It is, after all, British cooking that has been specified. That thing that assists you hardly qualifies as a Scotsman, much less an Englishman."

I covered my mouth to conceal my laughter. I had not expected such a meek-looking gentleman to possessed such a barbed wit. O'Malley and Harrison grinned at each other, then quickly recorded the exchange in their notebooks.

MacTavish's expression went from jovial to dark. "How dare you impugn the pedigree of my invention! It is, in fact, more British than you are."

At that remark, a hush fell over the crowd, as if we all expected an imminent altercation.

"As a gentleman, I shall not give that last remark the dignity of a response," sniffed Fenimore, "The use of a contraption made in Britain does not make it British cooking. It is, in fact, a violation of the rules."

"Are you calling me a cheat?" MacTavish growled. His hands formed into fists as he stepped up to Fenimore and stood inches away from his rival.

"Is that a threat? That's no surprise, considering the uncouth Celtic ruffian that you are."

"Gentlemen!" interrupted a broad-shouldered man who pushed his way through the crowd to step between the feuding chefs. "Kindly cease this disturbance at once." Another well-built man accompanied him. Both wore the same tuxedo-like uniforms we had seen at the entrance, with the brass weapons evident in their sleeves.

"Disturbance?" responded Fenimore, arching his eyebrows. "The only disturbance has been the so-called music played by this man's machine."

"I'll show ye a disturbance," MacTavish snapped.

"Sirs, you must cease your bickering." the guard continued. "There'll be no fisticuffs here. You can settle your feud in the kitchen. Come now, everyone, move along."

A murmur went through the crowd; some of them began to step away.

"Mother Mary and Joseph," O'Malley remarked. "That was interesting, to say the least."

"Interesting, yes. Exciting, no?" I said, mimicking my mother's French accent.

O'Malley's eyes met mine. He seemed to be ready to say something. I cleared my throat. "Tom, here is some perfect material for your paper."

O'Malley nodded and followed Harrison as he approached Fenimore. "Sir," said Harrison. "Have you anything to say about Mr. MacTavish's challenge? Do you intend to file any appeals concerning his use of a machine as an assistant?"

"I'm sorry," Fenimore said, "But I'm not inclined to remain here in the presence of this barbarian. Come, Matilda, let's go." He took his female companion by the arm. The couple hurried off without another word, followed by their Oriental associate. This very civilized event was becoming more intriguing than I had anticipated.

Chef MacTavish, however, was not about to relinquish the limelight. "As to the matter of the contest, I wish to make a few remarks," he said, stepping forward.

"Mr. MacTavish" Tom began. "I'm sure the public is duly impressed by your automaton. What do the rules actually say about the use of a mechanical assistant?"

As the men spoke, I slipped past them and stepped closer to look at the automaton. I reached out a hand and touched the metal man's brass skin. I could feel the cold of the surface through the thin material of my glove. I wished I had brought my camera.

"Ione!" Emma called, startling me. "You missed some excellent beluga caviar. I must say, you're easy to find. I just head for the nearest ruckus, and there you are."

"We just witnessed the most notorious culinary rivalry in the United Kingdom," I explained. "Fergus MacTavish of Glasgow versus Sir Charles Fenimore of London."

"Oh, my," Emma said. "I assumed the gossip about their mutual loathing was exaggerated. You know how disingenuous journalists can be."

"I would take that to be a jibe on our profession, madam," Harrison said with a sly smile. "If it hadn't been delivered by such a lovely pair of lips."

Emma smiled and said. "Mr. O'Malley, is this rogue a friend of yours?"

I made a quick introduction.

"And where is Mr. Farrington?" Harrison said. "Will he be attending the Exhibition?"

"I'm afraid not. He had a hunting trip," Emma explained. "And though he invited me to accompany him, this is much more my sort of activity. And how are things at the Times, Mr. Harrison? Have you retired from the political desk?"

"My goodness no," he replied. "I'm covering this event as a favor for our editor. You seem to know a lot about me."

"I know about many things. Like the runaway car incident," Emma continued, "In which Mr. O'Malley saved a small child and his mother from certain death. Not to mention Ione."

"Now, now, Mrs. Farrington, it was just a case of misapplied brakes. And the child's mother was nowhere near."

"Our hero!" Harrison proclaimed, grabbing Tom's arm and raising it up as if he were a champion prize fighter.

Tom slipped away from his friend's grasp, flushed with embarrassment.

"As for you, Mrs. Farrington," Harrison continued in his deep, melodious voice, "How are you enjoying our fair city?"

As she was about to reply, a loud squawk interrupted her. All four of us turned to see MacTavish make his grand exit, with Angus once again providing musical accompaniment.

"That is just awful," Emma clapped her hands over her ears. "No offense, Mr. O'Malley."

"None taken," Tom said. He leaned in close to me and whispered, "I'd forgotten how amusing things can be when I'm around you."

I call to a young Chinese serving girl for a cup of tea.
Illustration by Suzanne Stewart

Chapter 5. An Expedient Escort

As the crowds around us parted, I once again noted the delicious fragrances all around us. "I have been at the Exposition for several hours," I complained, "And have not tried even a morsel of this fine food."

"Nor have I," Tom replied with a smile.

"It's a shame you didn't get a chance to try the caviar," Emma said. "Que c'est délicieux!"

"I quite agree," Harrison added. "The greatest tragedy, however, was the thought of you eating alone, madam. I would have been happy to accompany you."

Emma smiled sweetly in response.

"I would have never expected so much rivalry in the cooking world," Harrison continued. "It's been more dramatic than the most contentious session of Parliament."

"Yes, the culinary world is intensely competitive," Emma said.

I consulted the clock embedded in the side of my purse. "It's nearly time for the evening banquet where I'm to give my speech. I should arrive a bit early to take my seat."

"The banquet hall is that way," Tom said, consulting the map.

As we headed down the promenade, Harrison lit his pipe and said, "Are you nervous, Professor D?"

Before I could speak, Emma answered for me. "Oh, piffle. Ione is always prepared. At school, she would practice her speeches so many times that even I knew them by heart."

We followed the flow of people down the hall and up a broad stairwell. At the top of the stairs, we met a dignified gentleman clad in the ubiquitous black tuxedo. His salt-and-pepper hair was matched by a well-trimmed mustache. "Invitations, please?"

I withdrew the credentials from my purse and handed it to him. His eyes lit up.

"Ah, Professor D, we've been awaiting you. Is this gentleman your escort?" He looked directly at Tom, who reacted with a look of surprise.

Emma mouthed the words, "I told you."

"Why, yes," O'Malley replied. "I'm the professor's escort." He grinned at Harrison. "Sorry, old chum. I've been promoted."

"Good for you, old chap!" Harrison gave O'Malley a playful slap on the shoulder. Mrs. Farrington," he said, offering his arm to Emma, "Will you do me the honor?"

"I'd be delighted."

"Mind your p's and q's now," Harrington called as the maître 'd led us away.

"That was meant for you, Ione," Tom said with a grin.

We followed the mustached gentleman into a large space filled with tables, many of them already occupied. The dining hall encompassed a large part of the second-floor balcony. A splendid feast was being prepared in our midst. He led us to the head table, situated on a raised platform by the farthest wall, then bowed and departed.

The ladies were already seated, with the men standing behind or close by. I was familiar with them from my prior research: young Lord Battenham, the King's third cousin, Sir Clive Young, the Lord Mayor of London, Cardinal Finchley of the Church of England, and Dame Leonora Eldridge of the Epicurean Society.

We took our places at the extreme end. Leonora was seated to our immediate left. I introduced myself and Tom.

"Pleased to meet you both. This is my husband Niles. Are you enjoying your visit to London?"

"Immensely." Tom and I took our seats. The other gentlemen followed suit. "Dame Leonora, I must commend your organization on a splendid exhibition."

"Thank you, though the real thanks must go to King Edward. Sadly, His Majesty was unable to attend tonight. But he will be present for the cooking contest finale two days hence."

"I am very much looking forward to it."

"As am I. It will be a great privilege to judge the greatest chefs in Britain."

"How exciting! Though I don't envy having to make such a difficult decision."

"I'm sure you would be quite competent, Professor D. Your friend, Mrs. Farrington, sent me your book; I was quite impressed. If you'd be so kind to sign my copy..." she opened her enormous handbag and pulled out my book, a quill pen and a tiny bottle of ink.

"I'd be delighted." I was impressed by her preparedness and Emma's boldness. I signed my name on the flyleaf, noticing how O'Malley beamed with pride. As I handed the book back to Leonora, I saw Emma smiling and nodding from the press table. I shot her a scolding look.

For the first time, I had butterflies thinking of my upcoming speech. Perhaps it was because of the presence of Tom and Emma.

Like everything we'd seen so far at the Exposition, the banquet was both grand and innovative. By now most of the tables were occupied. The diners wore exquisitely fashionable dress, men in hand-tailored suits and women in long gowns. At the press table, however, the reporters wore suits and dresses of a more frugal nature. Emma stood out among them. She wore her perfectly matched ensemble with an elegance I could never hope to replicate.

Numerous servers, mostly boys in their late teen years, pushed wheeled carts loaded with dishes of all descriptions. Girls rushed around bearing a variety of drinks. I counted seven entrées: Broiled beef stew, halibut, lobster, duck, kidney pie, a turkey baked in clay, and a roast pig. There were smaller carts loaded with side dishes such as potatoes and other vegetables. I noted that most of these portable tables incorporated a container of burning oil beneath its tray.

As discreetly as I could manage, I got my notepad from my purse and began jotting down details to later share with my students.

"Halibut," called a young server. "Steamed halibut, fresh from the North Sea."

"What do you fancy, Miss D?" Tom asked.

"It is a difficult decision," I replied. "Ah, there's the young man with the roasted duck." I waved at him. He nodded and headed toward our table.

"There you are, madam," the waiter said as he sliced into the bird and placed a generous helping on my plate. He also gave me a scoop of the accompanying side dish: a vegetable medley featuring that American delicacy, wild rice.

"I'll try the halibut," O'Malley called out, as another young man approached with the fish. As additional carts came by he also requested roast beef and lobster. I noticed Leonora giving him a disapproving glance. She and her husband had chosen just one entree each. Despite my better judgment, I signaled to a boy who was passing by with a cart laden with a whole roast pig. "I would love to try some of that," I said. "Would you like some, Tom?"

"Good heavens, no," he grinned. "I've got more than enough."

For a moment I banished my speech to the back of my mind as I savored the exquisite breast of duck, with its delicate citrus sauce. I jotted down my impressions of the dish, in hopes of duplicating it in the future.

As the serving girls returned, this time with pastries and coffee, Dame Leonora leaned in close to me. "We'll give the guests 15 minutes to get their desserts, and then it will be time for your speech, Professor."

"Thank you," I looked out over the room. There wasn't a vacant table in the place.

"Are you OK?" whispered O'Malley.

I nodded. "Is that girl serving tea?"

He followed my gaze to a slender, dark-haired girl currently passing between us and the press tables. "You mean her? The one with the big silver pot? Oh, miss!"

O'Malley waved to the girl and managed to catch her eye. She was currently serving an elderly lady in a purple dress. She finished filling that woman's cup then set out in our direction, leaving the lady's male companion holding out his empty cup with a surprised look on his face.

As we watched her struggle up the steps to the platform where we sat, O'Malley remarked, "Goodness, she's just a child; she can barely carry that pot."

I sighed. "To be working so hard at her age, I suspect she has endured many challenges in her young life."

O'Malley chuckled. "The most pressing challenge being not to spill on the guests."

The serving girl's shiny black hair was pulled back in a bun. Her large dark eyes, with their Oriental cast, were bewitching in her pale face, complementing her tiny nose and mouth. Her speech, however, was quite British. "Would you fancy some tea, ma'am?"

"Yes, please," I moved my cup and saucer to the edge of the table. "Tell me, child, what is your name?"

With her brow furrowed in concentration as she poured, she answered, "It's Lily, ma'am."

"What a pretty name!" I smiled.

"Thank you, ma'am," she stammered. She regained her composure and turned to O'Malley. "And you, sir?"

"Please," he said, moving his cup under the spout of the teapot.

Lily filled O'Malley's cup. "Enjoy your evening, sir and ma'am." She managed to curtsey while holding the heavy pot.

"Thank you," I said. "When you have a chance, might I trouble you for some sugar?"

"What've I told you?" A portly matron in a white frock rushed over to our table. "Serve the folks in order! You left that gentleman sitting with an empty cup in his hand."

"I'm sorry," the girl muttered and hurried away.

"It was my fault," I told the woman. "I will be speaking shortly, and I needed – "

"Don't go defending her, miss," The matron interrupted. "That little coolie girl should have had the common sense to serve your table first. Where'd she get off to now?"

"Don't be too harsh with her," said O'Malley. "She's doing her best."

"Leave her to me, sir. I know what those people are like. Enjoy your meal." She stormed off, muttering, "That's the last time we're hiring a bloody chink."

"Horrible woman," I said to O'Malley.

A moment later, the girl returned from the other direction with a blue and white china bowl full of sugar. "My apologies, ma'am," she said.

"No, I'm sorry," I replied. "Thank you."

Once again the girl curtsied and departed, ignoring the glare of the matron from across the room.

I stirred in the sugar and took a grateful sip. The heat of the tea soothed my throat, which was still sore from practicing my speech on my journey here. I glanced once again at the clock in my purse. It was just about time for me to speak.

Leonora leaned over to me and said, "My dear, it is time for your introduction." She looked at her notes and furrowed her brow. "How shall I pronounce your name?"

"It's Dfrdwy," I said.

"It's quite deficient in vowels," she remarked.

"You're welcome to introduce me by my pen name, Ione D."

She nodded, then made her way to the podium, whereupon she picked up and rang a silver hand bell several times until the diners fell silent.

"It is my great pleasure," she began, "To introduce a young lady whose work has taken the culinary world by storm.

In the few short months since its publication, her *History of British Cooking* has appeared in bookstores in a dozen nations and has been translated into five languages. I was seated next to her during our lovely meal, and I must say she is as charming and intelligent as she is beautiful. May I present our keynote speaker, Professor Ione D!"

Professor Ione D. & the Epicurean Incident

It was the handsome young man who had been eyeing me
during my speech, escorting a beautiful girl.
Illustration by José Cardeñas

Chapter 6. An Acclaimed Address

The audience greeted me with enthusiastic applause as I stepped up to the podium. It was a great honor, but it only served to make me more nervous. I forced my mind to focus on my goal, much as I'd learned to focus on the target while practicing archery under my father's tutelage. This may seem a strange comparison, but I have found both disciplines to utilize similar mental techniques.

I cleared my throat as delicately as possible and began.

"Good evening, ladies and gentlemen. It is with great honor and humility that I come here today. I am but a scholar. I merely record and extol the accomplishments of others, such as the culinary marvels achieved by those present.

"As a professional educator, it is my good fortune to teach the kind of bright, motivated young ladies who will help to lead our society. At Margaret Gallard College, they study many subjects, but by far their favorite is one that is not on the curriculum, that of romance." I was gratified to hear the audience respond with polite laughter.

"In our youth, our minds may sometimes become fixed on the matters of the heart, but some forms of passion subside, and others will enthrall us for a lifetime. For me, fine food is such a passion. Here the art of cooking marries the science of nutrition to create a thing of beauty and love, a thing which bonds families together. Although I spent much of my childhood in embassies where we enjoyed meals by some of the finest cooks, the simple dinners my mother prepared were those which I remember most fondly. It was all the better because she allowed me to work with her in the kitchen at an early age, and was always patient in teaching me her skills. Meals and dinners do more than sustain us, they make for great memories.

"As for remembrance, the history of romance is well taken care of. We have the great writers such as Shakespeare, Austen, and Dickinson to show us how a basic human need can be elevated to something that is almost ethereal. But what of humankind's other great love, food? Here we turn to the history of cooking, which in comparison to romance, is sadly unheralded. Yet food can be an inspiration in equal measure to romance. Good food nourishes not just the body but the soul; the sublime flavors of a sauce; the heartiness of meat roasted to perfection, the varied texture of vegetables sautéed to just the right degree of tenderness."

One of the techniques I use to maintain my confidence while speaking is to move my gaze around the audience and to concentrate on their faces as if I were speaking to them one on one. I resisted the urge to linger on my friend Emma, who was smiling and nodding as I spoke. Beside her sat Harrison, a pipe clenched in his teeth. Further back was Sir Fenimore with Matilda, a faint smile on his face as he listened. If MacTavish was present, I did not see him.

Situated to the left of this couple, was a table occupied by a mixed group of people who appeared to be in their mid-twenties. Among them was a young man who, unlike most of the audience, was not focused on me. Rather, his eyes wandered over the crowd. He was quite handsome, with chiseled features, black wavy hair, and piercing blue eyes. I must have lingered a moment too long because his eyes met mine and my mind went blank for an instant, almost causing me to lose my place. Luckily my notes were well-organized, and I was able to continue without a discernible pause. When I looked back once more, he was smiling at me but I refused to acknowledge his attention.

As I concluded, and the applause commenced, I thanked them, gave a small bow and returned to my seat. It seemed as if someone else had delivered the speech, not I, and yet I felt a serene satisfaction that this task was finished, for better or for worse.

As I returned to my place at the table, I was delighted to see a delicate china plate containing my very favorite dessert, a mill-feuille pastry. "Tom, you remembered!"

He nodded and took both my hands in his. "Well done, Ione! Your analogy of food and romance was brilliant. As the saying goes, the way to a man's heart is through his stomach."

"Thank you. But as for a man's heart, surely the ribcage would be a more direct route," I laughed.

"You have the most mischievous sense of humor," O'Malley replied. Our eyes locked together, maybe a trifle too long.

I tore my gaze from his and gave him an innocent smile before turning to my dessert. "If this pastry tastes as good as it looks, it should be an unparalleled delight!" I was just digging into the delicate crust with its perfectly sweet icing when I heard voices raised in anger.

"I merely noted that your cooking displays a lack of imagination," said MacTavish in his thick brogue. "If you interpret my remark as a slight upon your puny intelligence, so be it!"

"Are you accusing me of deafness as well? Because I heard the insult quite distinctly!" shouted Fenimore.

O'Malley watched as Harrison and several others from the press table excused themselves and went to observe the fracas now occurring in the rear of the hall. He sighed. "I've barely touched my dessert and they cause another commotion. My regrets, Ione, please excuse me."

"Of course," I nodded, turning back to my sweet pastry.

Tom grabbed his notebook and hurried toward the altercation. I noted that the press table had emptied, except for Emma, who glanced up at me, and then toward Tom.

"Excuse me, Mr. and Mrs. Mr. Eldridge." I rose from my seat and went to join my friend.

"Such scandalous behavior from grown men," I heard Leonora remark.

"Come along, Emma," I said, taking her by the hand. "If the two men resort to fisticuffs, we may be required to administer first aid."

"Brilliant!" she replied.

"In my country, we would settle this like men," MacTavish was saying.

"Your country?" Fenimore shot back. "If you do not consider yourself British, perhaps you do not belong in this competition."

"Now, now, gentlemen!" A portly balding man wearing a ribbon that said 'OFFICIAL' pushed his way through the crowd. "There is no need for such unpleasantness. We don't want to spoil such a splendid evening, do we?"

"Mr. Wagstaffe, I demand an apology from this uncouth barbarian," Fenimore insisted.

"If you're going to behave like schoolboys, we may need to send you to the woodshed," Wagstaffe responded, causing a titter of laughter from the spectators. "I daresay you should both apologize, to each other, and to the fine people in this room."

To my surprise, both chefs acquiesced to Wagstaffe's authority. The two men made subdued apologies and the argument was ended.

As I'd expected, the reporters closed in and assailed them with urgent, shouted questions. Once again, Fenimore refused to answer and pushed his way through the crowd and out of the dining hall, but MacTavish was happy to hold court.

"Such a shame," Emma said. "Just when things were beginning to get interesting."

I had to chuckle at her remark. We returned to the press table. While we waited for Tom and Harrison to finish their journalistic duties, we stopped young Lily for a quick a refill of our teacups.

"Poor girl," Emma said. "I wonder how much they're paying her."

"Surely not much," I said.

"I hope you ladies have not tired of fine food and drink," Harrison said as he and Tom rejoined us, "Because there's a wine tasting on level one, featuring the best vintages from around the world." We readily accepted and proceeded there with the two men. The hall was quite crowded.

"Look, Gerry," O'Malley said, "Is that Admiral Blakey, talking to the lady in the blue dress?"

"It is indeed," Harrison agreed. "Perhaps he has something to say about the recent Chinese conflict. If you'll excuse us, ladies, a journalist's work is never done. Come along, old chap." He motioned to O'Malley, and they departed.

With the men thus occupied, Emma and I circulated through the room, mingling with the other guests. I was surprised at how many people she knew by name. She was a most gracious companion, introducing me to each of them, many of whom requested my autograph. It was a great thrill to meet so many of the people whom I had only known by reputation, and an even greater thrill to learn that they respected my work.

I must confess that I found myself looking around for the handsome dark-haired man who had caught my eye in the audience. As the crowd was mostly comprised of couples, I expected he would be easy to spot, but he was nowhere to be seen.

"You seem to be a trifle distracted," Emma said. "Are you looking for someone?"

"No, nobody. I'm just feeling a bit overwhelmed."

Emma did not seem convinced.

Once aroused, my curiosity was impossible to ignore. Who was he? Was he a dignitary? Was he part of the royal family?

Just as I had put the mysterious man out of my mind, I saw him, standing and conversing with Dame Leonora and her husband. At his side was a tall, fair-skinned brunette who exuded loveliness; her hair was dark and curly like his, cascading down her back, where it met with her elegant sky blue dress.

"Do you know them?" I asked Emma. "That attractive young couple over there."

"Hmm, no, I don't," she said. "Let us go introduce ourselves, shall we?"

I shrugged. "It's up to you." At that moment, an Austrian duke in full dress uniform approached Emma, greeting her like an old friend. After the introductions, and the explanations – they had met on a river cruise of the Rhine – he was off to rejoin his wife. I looked around for the young couple, but they had disappeared.

Though Emma was quite chatty on the taxi ride back to the hotel, I was rather drowsy, having imbibed a bit more than usual. I fell asleep mere minutes after lying down on my bed.

The next morning, I felt refreshed and eager to return to the Exposition. Tom and Emma were both waiting for me in the lobby, and we hailed a cab – this time it was a motorized one – to the Crystal Palace.

"Although I'm fond of horses, I must say the trend toward motorcars is a change for the better," said O'Malley as we rode. "I spent a lot of time in my youth shoveling up after them."

I laughed at his straightforwardness. "Indeed, though I expect the automobile to have its own set of challenges."

As we rode, Emma and Tom chatted quietly, while I reviewed my copy of the Exhibition's souvenir guidebook. There were so many fascinating activities. More than anything, I was looking forward to the All-Britain Royal Culinary Competition. It was a two-day affair, with the most celebrated cooks from around the country.

When we arrived, Mr. Wagstaffe greeted us, accompanied by a well-dressed young male assistant. "Professor D, I'm so glad we found you! One of our judges, Mrs. White from Surrey, had an unfortunate accident and is now in hospital. We need to make a last-minute replacement."

"Accident?" O'Malley asked. "What has happened?"

Wagstaffe lowered his voice "It was a rather embarrassing incident. We employ a number of boys to scoop up the waste the horses leave behind, and cart it away. Somehow a quantity of said waste was deposited on the walkways leading to the dinosaur statuary. Mrs. White slipped and fell on the pavement."

"My goodness," I said. "I hope she's alright."

"Thankfully her injuries were not serious," Wagstaffe replied. "But at the moment, she is in considerable pain."

"Horse manure on the walkways?" O'Malley said. "I wonder how that happened."

Wagstaffe shrugged. "Since carriages are prohibited from traversing that area, we have reported the incident to the authorities as a possible act of vandalism. I must stress that the Epicurean Society is in no way responsible."

"Of course," O'Malley nodded as he jotted down a few lines in his notebook. "Though perhaps they might assist with the poor lady's cleaning bill."

The Exhibition manager shot him a disapproving glance. "Now as to Mrs. White's replacement. Although in principle, all judges should be British, we have not been able to find anyone with the proper credentials. Professor D., would you be willing to serve in this capacity?"

"Me? I am quite honored, but..." I looked at Tom and Emma.

"No don't worry about abandoning us," Emma said. "Tom will be busy with his journalistic duties, and I will certainly be able to find something to occupy myself."

"Absolutely," Tom agreed. "The success of the Exhibition rests upon your lovely and capable shoulders."

"Such flattery!" I laughed. "Thank you both for your confidence." I looked at the official. "Yes, Mr. Wagstaffe, I would be happy to be a judge."

Wagstaffe clapped his hands in triumph. "Splendid! Kindly come with me; I will give you a brief introduction to the requirements, and then escort you to your first judging."

"Farewell for now, Ione, and good luck," O'Malley bowed quickly and departed.

"As for you, Mrs. Farrington," Wagstaffe said, "To compensate you for the loss of your companion, the society will take care of all your meals."

"I greatly appreciate that," she replied, "I'll start with breakfast. Ione, I shall see you at the cooking contest."

"Excellent." To his assistant, Wagstaffe said, "Please escort Mrs. Farrington to my personal table in the staff dining area, and make sure she is well taken care of."

"Yes, sir!" The young man left with my friend in tow.

At the management office, I signed a document promising to be strictly impartial, whereupon Wagstaffe presented me with a ribbon that said 'JUDGE,' which I proudly pinned on my blouse.

My first destination was the judges' table at Contest Station Number 1. There were four of these, situated in various places along the broad promenade of the Crystal Palace. At each location, they had set up temporary kitchen facilities and enough chairs for a small audience and a panel of three judges.

In this first round of the contest, 64 cooks from all around the Kingdom would compete in groups of four. This first round of contests would take up an entire day. The resulting 16 semi-finalists would move on to the next round to be held the following morning. The final four would compete for top honors in front of thousands of attendees in the Palace's Concert Hall.

"No wonder there are so many judges," I remarked to Wagstaffe.

"Indeed. Finding qualified judges has been a major undertaking. Thank you again, Professor D." He smiled, showing crooked teeth.

"You are most welcome," I replied. My heart beat faster with anticipation. I had thought that my official duties over, but that was not to be. I had found myself at the center of the Exhibition's pivotal event.

Professor Ione D. & the Epicurean Incident

The first round of chefs compete in the All-Britain Royal
Culinary Competition.
Illustration by José Cardeñas

Chapter 7. The Competition Commences

At Station One, a man and woman were already waiting at the judges' table. "Professor D.," Wagstaffe began, "This is Mr. Oliver Talbot of the Gastronomical Society of Liverpool, and Mrs. Nell Grace, manager of the Grace Cooking Schools. Mr. Talbot and Mrs. Grace, Professor D. will be taking Mrs. White's place." Both rose from their seats to greet me. "And now, I must be on my way."

The three of us exchanged pleasantries while we awaited the beginning of the contest. Despite the early hour, the Exhibition was already teeming with guests. The gray skies over London were visible through the transparent walls and roof of the exhibition hall. Shortly after my arrival, the rain began to fall with a gentle patter on the glass.

People began taking their seats in the spectator area. I was happy to see Emma sitting front and center, chatting with an older lady I did not recognize.

"Now, Professor D.," said Talbot. "I trust you know how this contest will proceed."

"Yes," I replied. "We judge four dishes per session, rating each on a scale of one to ten."

"Four sessions in all today," Talbot said. "Besides this one, they're scheduled for ten AM, two PM, and four."

"That will be a lot of tasting," I said.

"Indeed," said Mrs. Grace. "But one's palate becomes accustomed to making subtle distinctions in taste and texture."

"And presentation is important as well," Talbot added. "A great dish should look attractive on the plate."

"I agree," I said, "Though I am uncertain as to how much weight to assign..."

The sound of shouting interrupted me, and we all turned to see the source of the disturbance. Two of the Exhibition's uniformed security guards were guiding – almost dragging – a slight, plainly dressed man with a head of thick white hair.

"I didn't do nothin' wrong!" he cried. "I paid my way in, do ya want to see my ticket? I was just passin' out lit'rature like anybody else 'round here."

"Another Irish agitator," sniffed Talbot.

"Why is that a problem?" I asked.

"This is neither the time nor the place," Talbot said. "A visitor's pass doesn't give one the right to pass out propaganda on the promenade."

"Ah, here is our first group of contestants," said Mrs. Grace, who was clearly anxious to change the subject.

Professor Ione D. & the Epicurean Incident

For a moment I was puzzled, as there were not four but eight people filing in, until I remembered that each chef was allowed one assistant. Six of the eight were men, and most looked to be around my parents' age.

One of the chefs was a handsome young gentleman. When I realized who it was, it took me a moment to catch my breath. It was the same dark-eyed man who had caught my eye during my talk.

His assistant was his pretty young companion from the previous evening. I felt a pang of disappointment and admonished myself at once. As I looked his way, he shot me his intense gaze for a brief moment. I had to marvel at his audacity.

Looking through the printed schedule for the competition, I determined that the roguish young man was Neville Montague of Brighton. The assistants' names were not included.

Despite the fact that these two were younger than the other contestants, they prepared their meal with great efficiency. Montague transferred items with ease from one skillet to another on the gas-fired burner that each entrant was provided. His assistant chopped the ingredients and handed it to him without being asked. I was impressed that this young couple was the first to finish.

According to the schedule, the theme of the first session that morning was breakfast. Dieu merci, I thought. In my haste, I had not had a chance to eat that morning. By this time, the wonderful smells were drawing the attention of passers-by, and the chairs that had been provided for the audience were almost all occupied.

All the breakfasts being prepared were hearty ones. Three of the dishes contained sausage: two versions of bangers and mash, and one bubble and squeak with a side of sausage. The fourth was a stottie cake stuffed with eggs and bits of bacon.

Montague's entry, the 'bubble and squeak' was a surprising one. This is a dish that is normally assembled from the leftovers of a previous evening's dinner. For this event, the ingredients were freshly prepared, with the goal of providing the typical mixture of contrasting tastes that is achieved by using whatever one has in the larder.

"I'm familiar with all of these chefs," Talbot remarked, "Except for this Montague fellow."

"I know his family," Mrs. Grace said, "They run an Inn near Brighton Harbour."

"That's an unconventional choice he made," Talbot said. "I myself would have played it safe this first round. On the other hand, not all of these teams have the advantage of having worked together all their lives, as he and his sister have."

"His sister?" I blurted out, a bit too loudly. The faux pas caused my cheeks to redden. Thankfully, the other judges seemed not to notice.

"Yes, she is quite lovely, isn't she?" said Mrs. Grace. "I understand she is betrothed to the eldest son of the Duke of Beaufort. Her brother, however, is quite the eligible bachelor."

"I see," I remarked. "No wonder they get along so well."

One by one the contestants approached the table and served us each a portion of his creation. Though all of the entries were tasty, none rose to the level of the "bubble and squeak," which had none of the heaviness that is so common in fried foods. Each of us awarded him eight points, which meant Montague had won this bout and would advance to the next round.

As the day went on, I was regretful that, between my duties as keynote speaker and now as a judge, I would have little free time to explore the Exhibition. I was excited to see the latest cooking-related inventions. Still, I took the opportunity to join Emma to peruse a few of the booths in between the multiple food-judging sessions.

"They are all very interesting," my friend remarked. "But many of them strike me as impractical. For example, the steam-powered potato peeler?"

"The device had its merits, perhaps, but as for its inventor, what an unpleasant man! Say, look over there! A mechanical egg-cracker! I would love to see it in operation."

"It can crack up to a dozen at a time," the exhibitor was explaining to a small audience. "You simply place the eggs in this tray, pull down this lever, and voila!" We watched as a padded rack above the tray descended then grabbed and lifted all the eggs. An array of sharp circular knives neatly removed the end of each egg, then poured the contents in a chamber below.

"It's simply marvelous! I exclaimed. "My mother would love it!"

"I miss her pastries," Emma commented.

I wrote the man a cheque and put in an order for one to be shipped to my parents' home in Washington, DC. *Mama will be so surprised!*

I had three more sessions that day, each of which brought in four new contestants to each of the four stations. Such redundancy was required to handle the large number of entrants in the limited time allotted to the contest.

For this second session, the theme was pastries that could be served as a main course. In this group, two of the cooks were men and two were women. One of the women was quite tall, with short sandy hair. Until I consulted the biographical notes they had supplied us, I had mistaken her for a man. Her assistant was an elderly gentleman who seemed to be trying his best to stay out of her way. The woman's name was Agnes Richards and she hailed from the Denton Culinary Academy in Manchester.

Emma was once again a prominent member of the audience. I noticed she had procured a glass of red wine, which made me envious until in the midst of a spirited conversation with the lady next to her, she spilled half of it all over her light blue frock. Dear Emma simply laughed and left her seat. When she didn't return promptly, I wasn't overly concerned, as Emma had probably encountered someone she knew and become immersed in conversation.

While we waited for the dishes to cook, a serving girl brought us tea for the traditional "elevenses." Grace and Talbot occupied themselves in idle chatter, but I was in no mood for conversation. I had grown tired of sitting and to make things worse, the rain had cleared up. It was a beautiful sunny day beyond the walls of the Crystal Palace, and I longed to be outdoors.

My boredom ended when a woman cried out. It seemed that two men had been arguing, and one pushed the other into a group of ladies who had been passing by. The first man turned on his heels and disappeared down the corridor. I didn't see his face, but the shock of unruly gray hair was unmistakable. It was the vendor who been so rude to Emma and me.

When the second man got to his feet, I was even more surprised. He looked toward our station and stared at me for a moment before he hurried away.

"Who in blazes was that?" asked Talbot.

"His name is Lang Min. He's the Chinaman who assists Sir Fenimore," said Mrs. Grace. "I don't know who the ruffian was who knocked him over. What a frightful impression to give to a guest in our country."

"The other man is also a foreigner," I said. "I encountered him in the vendor area – a most unpleasant fellow."

Finally, the food was ready and we were able to taste what we had been smelling all this time. There was a fish pie with leeks and potatoes and two variants of the Cornish pasties, all of which were reasonably tasty. Once again it was the unconventional entry that stood out above the rest. Agnes Richards' dish was a mince pie that proved to be truly scrumptious. Rather than meat, it contained some kind of fowl which was definitely not domesticated.

"Partridge," Mrs. Grace remarked as if answering my mental question. "Quite tender!"

"And tasty," Talbot added. "Rather like an Indian curry. Does it fit within the parameters of British cooking?"

"Technically speaking," I said, "India is part of the British Empire."

"Quite right," Talbot agreed.

We awarded her a total of 28 points, one point more than her nearest competitor.

Emma approached as we were getting up from the table. She had managed to remove the wine stain completely. I was not surprised that she was already acquainted with Mrs. Grace and Mr. Talbot.

"The contest schedule's mid-day break is only until 2 PM," Emma said. "Hardly enough time for a full dinner. Perhaps a light lunch?"

"After sampling all those dishes, I could hardly manage a dinner. But I would enjoy a taste of something sweet perhaps."

We quickly found a stall that was serving beignets with powdered sugar. "Not as good as the ones your mother makes," Emma commented. "But tasty nonetheless."

"Agreed. By the way," I said, "I saw your little mishap, and I'm happy to see you were able to keep the wine from staining that lovely dress of yours. Did you use seltzer water?"

"Yes, and I had to go all the way to the kitchens to find some. Would you believe they actually posted a guard at the entry door? Luckily an acquaintance of mine from the Epicurean Society happened by to vouch for me."

"Ah. I noticed that it took you quite some time to return."

"Oh, it wasn't because of that. While I was in the kitchens I... Say, would you mind stopping at that sandwich shop? The beignets were delicious but I would like a bit more."

"Certainly. I will sample their tea at least."

Sadly, the tea was disappointing, neither as fresh or as strong as I like it. Still, it was tolerable, and I sipped while Emma enjoyed some cucumber sandwiches.

"You were telling me about something that happened in the kitchens," I said.

"Right. I'm embarrassed to speak of it because it was probably nothing. Do you remember that Oriental fellow that was with Fenimore when he had that big row with MacTavish?"

"Yes. I understand he serves as Fenimore's *sous chef*."

"I was dashing around here and there, looking for seltzer, and when I encountered him at one of the tables mixing up some sort of sauce. When he saw me, he immediately rolled up this cloth case which I assume held his spices. He began shouting at me in broken English, accusing me of being a spy for MacTavish and trying to steal his ideas."

"Curious," I replied, nodding.

"There was a guilty air about him." She grimaced. "I noticed something else that was odd. He was wearing rubberized gloves, like a factory worker. Why on earth would he do that?"

"That is odd. Some spices may sting if one forgets and rubs one's eyes. Though that would seem to be an excessive precaution. Speaking of suspicious occurrences, I have one for you as well. While you were gone, there was an altercation between Fenimore's assistant and another man."

"Really? That's quite a coincidence.'"

"Perhaps. The most interesting thing was whom he was arguing with. It was that rude vendor, the man with the potato machine."

"Did you catch anything they were saying?"

"No, if they spoke at all, it was very brief. It may have as simple as a chance collision on the Promenade. In any case, the vendor seemed quite angry, and knocked the Chinese man to the floor before hurrying away."

"What a strange occurrence. I have been to cooking competitions before and I was concerned this one might be a bit dull. I had no idea it could be so dramatic."

"Indeed. Emma, I think something is afoot."

"That's my Ione!" Emma grabbed both my hands in hers and grinned. "I was dearly hoping we would find some mischief."

"Oh, Emma, I hope not," I sighed. "I'm sure there must be a logical explanation for all of this. But let's keep our eyes open, shall we?"

Soon thereafter the third round began. I was beginning to think Emma had been wrong about the possibility of trouble at such a genteel event – until yet another mishap occurred.

Professor Ione D. & the Epicurean Incident

Emma and I find a charming little tea-house in the
Exhibition Hall.
Illustration by Suzanne Stewart

Chapter 8. A Curious Coincidence

When the afternoon sessions commenced I was at Station Four, which was situated at the opposite end of the concourse from my location that morning. Here my fellow judges were from the food service industry. Whereas they were both polite enough, they took this event very seriously and were not given to idle chit-chat.

The degree of public interest had changed as well. There had been only a handful of spectators for the first event and a modest number for the second, but there were now hundreds of people clustered around the roped-off area in which we sat. The theme for this session was soups and stews, and each chef was provided a heating element for this purpose.

One of the contestants, a plump, grandmotherly lady, was trying to relight the burner at her table. All at once there was a massive pop and a shriek. The poor lady jumped in alarm and flew back towards the audience. People shouted, screamed, and looked on in horror as she fell to the floor, her frilly apron in flames.

I leapt from my seat at the judge's table, as I was nearest to her station. I grabbed the bucket of water at the edge of the cordoned-off area, almost colliding with a man in dark clothing who had also been rushing toward the scene.

"Mind where you're going!" cried the man.

I ignored him and dumped the contents of the bucket onto the woman's apron, causing her to cry out in surprise. "*Quelle horreur!*" I exclaimed. "Are you hurt?"

The woman replied with a fit of coughing. I squatted down next to her to look her over.

"Heavens no, dear, I'm fine," the woman sputtered. "I've just got the wind knocked out of me." She looked down at her scorched and tattered clothing. "Oh, bollocks! My lucky apron is ruined!"

"What a pity! But thank goodness that was all." Her injuries appeared to be confined to some abrasions on her arms and a shallow cut on the head.

"Please, folks, stand back!" A man with a medical bag and an exhibition badge pushed his way through the crowd, with a white-clad nurse close behind him. "Madam, are you alright?"

"Good gracious," the lady exclaimed, "All this fuss over me! I'm fine, thank you! God bless you, young lady for your quick thinking!"

Despite her protestations, the doctor persuaded her to come along to the infirmary for a checkup.

As I watched them escort her away, a voice from my left gave me a start. "You're quite the sensation today, aren't you Professor D?"

"Sensation? Heavens no, I wouldn't..." I stopped in mid-sentence as I realized that the man who was speaking, upon whom I had almost emptied the bucket of water, was the handsome Mr. Montague.

My mouth suddenly dry, it took me a moment to complete the thought. "I'd hardly call my actions sensational. Though I must apologize for almost colliding with you."

"You are forgiven. I applaud your boldness in taking action. My name is Neville Montague." He gave a quick bow. "I greatly enjoyed your speech last night, as well as your poise and self-assurance in this crisis. May I..." his eyes fell to my soaked blouse, "assist you?"

"Oh, my!" My cheeks flushed as I pulled a kerchief from my jacket pocket, and began furiously dabbing the wet fabric. I looked up to see him holding out his own handkerchief to me.

"Here." He patted the dry cloth on my cheeks and forehead.

Our eyes met and I quickly looked away. "Thank you." I felt an urgent need to say something. "I remember you from Round One. I must commend you for your innovative entry."

"I am honored," he replied with a nod. "Did you find it to be – "

His reply was cut short when Emma rushed in with her mouth wide in amazement. "Ione, you saved that woman's life!" Seeing Neville's startled reaction, she collected herself and said, "Please pardon my interruption. I don't believe we've been introduced."

"Mr. Montague, this is my friend from school, Mrs. Emma Farrington."

"The Conqueror's Tavern in Brighton, isn't it? I've heard good things about your restaurant."

"I'm pleased to hear my family's good reputation precedes me."

"I haven't had the pleasure of dining there. Regrettably, my husband and I don't make it to the coast very often." She continued with a barrage of questions about his family and their establishment, without pausing for breath. He responded to several with forced politeness, then discreetly interrupted her.

"Begging your pardon, Mrs. Farrington, Professor D. I must be off to prepare for the next round," He bowed quickly and departed, looking back to give me a wink.

I watched Montague depart, then said to Emma, "Why was he lingering around here when he should have been preparing for the next contest?"

"Don't be so suspicious. It's my fault he didn't go sooner. I did get a bit carried away with my questions."

Shortly thereafter, the unfortunate lady contestant returned, her ruined apron replaced with a new one, a bandage wrapped around her arm and some salve on the cut on her forehead. In the meantime, a repairman in overalls was just finishing a check of her station. "Got a crack in the gas line near the burner," I heard him say to the other judges. "She's a lucky woman; she coulda been blown to Kingdom Come."

Emma took her seat and the contest resumed as if nothing had happened. The only surprise was that O'Malley didn't appear sooner at the scene of the incident. I saw him on the sidelines speaking to one of the contest officials. There was, of course, no opportunity to speak with him. I promised myself to tell him later about the Chinese man and the vendor.

This time, the judging was a bit more difficult, if only because none of the entries were particularly outstanding. The winner was a broiled cod – tasty but unremarkable – from a sour-faced gentleman who nonetheless accepted his victory graciously. "I offer my humble thanks to His Majesty and England for making this possible."

The day's final session passed without incident. I was disappointed I hadn't had the opportunity to judge either MacTavish or Fenimore. Any of their creations were certain to be exquisite. Thinking of Fenimore brought my thoughts back to our recent encounters with the Chinese assistant. Was he up to something illegal? What was his connection, if any, to the potato chopper man?

I shook my head at my own suspicions. It was probably nothing. *This is not one of Emma's crime novels.*

When at last the final contest of the day was over, it was quite late in the afternoon.

"Thank you for staying with me," I said as I met Emma on the promenade. "It was reassuring to see a friendly face in the audience."

"It was my pleasure," she replied. "I suppose by now you must be feeling quite sated. But I would very much like to have a cup of tea, even if it is rather late."

I gave her a broad smile. "I would like nothing better. I might even have enough appetite to eat half a scone."

This being a culinary exhibition, it was not difficult to find a place to take tea. The Tareyton Tea Company had set up a charming tea-house at the extreme western end of the hall. We sat at a small table and ordered two cups of Earl Grey, which was a favorite of both of us.

"Out of all the food you sampled," she asked me, "which was your favorite?"

As I paused to consider her question, she interjected, "Was it the bubble and squeak?"

"Emma," I gave her a stern look because I knew what she was implying. "That was good, but no, my favorite was the mince pie from Miss Richards."

"And now that the contests are done for the day, what shall we do this evening?"

"Once again I am very sorry, but I have other commitments."

"What's that? A meeting with that delightful Montague fellow?"

"Emma, please," I adopted a tone of mock outrage, "I just met the man. Do you think me the type to throw myself at the first unmarried fellow I meet?"

"That depends..." she said, with a mischievous smile. "On whether he's handsome, charming and successful. If he's all three, you need to strike when the iron is hot."

I shook my head. "No, it's nothing so salacious. It's one of my duties as a literary guest. I've been scheduled to appear at Hollander's, the bookseller. Miss Miller, my publicist, has arranged for me to sit at a table and autograph copies of my book."

"Then I assume you could use an assistant, to manage the queue, hand you their books, make sure you have fresh ink for your pen, and collect calling cards from potential gentleman suitors."

"Emma, stop! You are incorrigible!" I laughed. "But to your kind offer, yes, I confess I was hoping you would volunteer. I would be most grateful to have your assistance and company."

The line was longer than I expected, and many of those waiting were holding brand new books. It was exhilarating to see that so many people wanted to get my autograph.

"Goodness, you've become quite a celebrity. Would you permit me a photograph?" It was O'Malley, standing next to my table with his usual wry smile. Harrison was away, chatting with a pretty girl in line.

Adopting a serious expression, I looked at Emma and said, "Would you call the guard, please?"

"I'll do no such thing!" To O'Malley, she said, "Of course Ione would be delighted to pose for you."

"Fine," I said. "Should I attempt a smile, or should I adopt a scholarly expression?"

"It is your choice," O'Malley said, "Though I prefer your smile. And please do not go, Mrs. Farrington. I would like you to be in the photograph as well."

"Oh, my! Do I look presentable?" Emma made a show of patting her hair into place, which was, as always, perfect.

O'Malley bent down and opened his satchel. "These new box cameras require much less time for exposure." He quickly mounted it on a tripod and prepared the flash powder. I gave him my best smile and waited for the dazzling light.

As I sat back in my seat, still struggling to blink away the after-image. Harrison said, "I would like a picture as well, please. If you would be so kind to indulge me, I would like an image of you speaking with one of your readers."

"Very well," I said. "If the next in line does not object."

"I would be honored," said a man's voice, and as my eyes focused I realized it was Neville Montague once again. His gaze was so disarming that I forgot to dip my pen; it scratched the page without leaving a mark.

"Oh, so sorry, sir!" Emma quickly dipped a pen into ink and exchanged it for the one I had been holding.

"How disappointing," he said. "I assumed that the professor was writing a message in invisible ink, for my eyes only."

"Such a charming sense of humor," I said. "Shall I address it to anyone in particular? I mean, is it for you, or is the book a gift?"

"It's for me," he said. There was an awkward pause as I was lost in his gaze for a moment. As I signed his book, Emma nudged me. I looked up just in time to be blinded again, this time by the flash of Harrison's camera.

"So we meet again, Mr. Montague," Emma said. "I heard that you won yet another round of the contest. What was your entry, if I may ask?"

"Thank you," he said. "It was a beef stew with mushrooms – a secret recipe that my family has passed down for generations."

I looked past him and noticed that O'Malley was still standing nearby. He appeared to be engaged in conversation with Harrison, though for a moment he glanced in my direction. I gave him a smile and he looked away.

I turned back to the man standing in front of me. "Very well, Mr. Montague." Trying to maintain a professional tone, I added, "Thank you for your patronage." I passed the book back to him, its cover still open to give the ink a chance to dry.

Montague accepted the book and gently blew on the page, never taking his eyes off of me. "I would like to make one further request," he said. "After this event is concluded, would you join me for a late supper?"

"Thank you, Mr. Montague," I said, "But you know as well as I, that since you are still a contestant and I am still a judge, there is a chance I may be judging your next entry tomorrow. Therefore I must decline."

"I understand." He closed the book, but his eyes remained on me. Out of the corner of my eye, I saw O'Malley lingering as he packed his photographic equipment. He shot Montague a look of suspicion, which the dark-haired man did not acknowledge.

"Ione," Tom said. "If anyone should present a problem for you, kindly let me know, and I shall inform the book shop's management."

"Thank you Mr. O'Malley, but I am quite capable. Next in line, please?"

"Thank you, Professor Dfrdwy," Montague said, pronouncing my name perfectly. He gave a quick bow and departed.

My mouth suddenly dry, I was about to ask Emma for a glass of water when a young female voice brought me back to my senses. "Professor D!" I realized she had said my name multiple times.

"Oh, I'm sorry, miss." I looked up at Emma, who was giving me one of her looks.

A pretty blonde school girl stepped forward. "Professor D," she gushed, "I want to be just like you when I grow up."

"That is most flattering," I smiled. I opened the book she handed me and began to sign it.

In the next instant, a loud boom made my heart leap from my chest. It was like indoor thunder followed by a rain of glass. My pen skipped, leaving a blotch of ink on the book. The girl gave an ear-splitting shriek, and I sprang to my feet and pulled her to safety under the awning of the book shop. *"Mon Dieu*, are you alright?"

The girl was crying hysterically. I realized she was covered with glass shards, as was everything in the promenade in front of us. People ran to and fro, screaming and shouting. A huge crowd was gathering, making it impossible to see what was in front of us.

"Look!" Emma pointed up at the ceiling, where a gaping hole had appeared above us, now open to the night sky.

"Come, dear, let me help." I pulled the sobbing little blonde closer and examined her. "It's just a few abrasions. You'll be fine."

"Ione!" cried Emma. "It's not just the glass! The stairway – it's gone!"

I jumped up on my chair for a better look. The ceiling wasn't all that had fallen; the stairway leading to the mezzanine had collapsed to the floor. The wrought-iron railings had snapped and were pulled partially off their moorings. "Tom, where are you?" I called. Where had he gone, and where was Montague?

"Help!" a man shouted. "My wife, she's not moving!"

Our mysterious assailant turns out to be a big fat goose.
Illustration by Kelly Morford

Chapter 9. A Mysterious Mishap

The long line that had awaited my signature evaporated as everyone moved to see what had occurred at the stairway. From my vantage point atop my chair, I could see the yawning gap in the roof but I couldn't tell what had caused it. Was it a bomb or projectile? The chair wobbled under my feet as I strained to see.

"Do you see Tom?" I called to Emma, who had scaled a nearby pedestal bearing a large potted plant.

"There, I see him!" She pointed at Tom's reddish hair protruding above the crowd.

"The camera!" Harrison's voice rang out. "Help me set it up, Tom!"

"Thank goodness," I sighed. I had feared the worst.

Relieved that O'Malley and his friend had not been harmed, I stepped off the chair and brushed off the seat with my gloved hand. The little blonde girl had disappeared but had forgotten her book. I prayed that no one had been seriously injured. As if in answer, two medics appeared bearing a woman – presumably the injured wife – away on a stretcher, awake and thankfully alive.

"It's been a right disaster, it has," said a voice to my right. It was the shop manager, Mr. Pennyworth, a slight little man in a dowdy suit. "The Exhibition, I mean. I'd wager that His Majesty will mount an investigation; if he doesn't, he should. There's been too many mishaps to be the product of chance."

"So you believe the incidents to be deliberate?" I asked. "Who would do such a thing, and for what purpose?"

"I don't rightfully know, but I'd first focus on the Irish. Those people have a grudge and I wouldn't put it past 'em to act on it."

"Curious though," I sighed. "Since it would only be to the detriment of their cause."

I didn't envy the authorities as they dealt with the situation, but soon they had moved the crowd back and roped off the area. Seated as we were at the table at the forefront of the store, we were afforded a prime view of the proceedings. Emma and I watched as they carried out a half- dozen more victims on stretchers.

"Thank heavens," Emma said, "It appears there was no loss of life."

"We can all be grateful for that," I agreed. "Mr. Pennyworth has been speculating whether this incident is tied to the others. It does seem a rather unlikely coincidence."

"So you think this has been the work of some kind of conspiracy? Criminal gangs perhaps?"

I laughed. "I don't know. I try to examine all the options like Sherlock Holmes would."

Mr. Pennyworth approached and said, "Professor, given the circumstances, they've asked us to close up for the evening."

"I completely understand. You've been a most gracious host. Could you please hold onto this book in case its owner returns? It was the little blond girl in the peach dress."

"You are most welcome, and I would be glad to."

"My goodness," Emma yawned as she glanced at her pocket watch. "It's well past ten. We should be on our way back to the hotel."

"Yes, definitely. My nerves are frazzled from all the excitement, and my limbs are all but numb from sitting so long. Would you accompany me on a stroll outdoors for some fresh air?"

"I'd love to," Emma said. "After all that excitement, a walk would be most relaxing."

We found ourselves heading down the walk to the lake that featured the dinosaur sculptures, now dark and foreboding in the moonlight.

"We're lucky for the clear night and the full moon to light our way," Emma said. "The gas lights do not extend far enough down the walk."

"Yes," I agreed. "Still, we must check our steps carefully. We don't want to hurt ourselves like Mrs. White did. I was glad to hear her injuries were not severe."

"I suspect it was more her pride that was wounded than anything," Emma laughed.

"And I can't imagine how one would get those stains out of one's dress!"

"Ione!" Emma whispered, grabbing me by the arm. "Do you see that dark figure ahead?"

"It looks like a child," I replied.

"It's rather late for a young person to be out unescorted. We should try to get closer and see if he needs our help."

"Ever the mother, aren't you?"

We quickened our pace. As we began close the gap between us, the mysterious person walked faster, which caused Emma and I hurry even more.

"Ione," Emma said, "I hope we're not frightening –"

All at once there was a terrible noise and a frightful flurry that made me jump and Emma shriek. A creature had charged out of the bushes, rushed past me and focused its wrath on my friend. She fled in alarm then fell to the ground as the heel of her shoe sank into the soft ground.

I let out a laugh when I saw that Emma's attacker was a big fat goose. "Shoo, go away!" I cried. "Or it's into the pot with you!"

The bird was not afraid. With a flurry of wings, it turned on me, biting at my feet with its big hard beak. I managed to open up my purse and retrieve a spray bulb filled with a harmless but irritating solution of water and cayenne pepper. When the mist reached the goose's face, it fell back, honking angrily, and retreated into the darkness.

"Are you hurt, Emma?" I extended a hand to help her up.

"No, just my pride," she chuckled. "Like the unfortunate Mrs. White."

"Do you ladies need any help?" The voice from behind startled me, even though it was so quiet and retiring that I thought for a moment I had imagined it.

"Only if you're a seamstress," said Emma, "because I'm sure my dress will need some mending."

I turned around to see a young girl in a black and white kitchen worker's uniform. Even in the dark, I could tell it was Lily, the Chinese girl who had served us earlier. "What are you doing here in the dark all by yourself?"

"My work is finished for the day, miss."

"Your family is not here to escort you?" I immediately regretted saying that. It was rude of me to ask such a forthright question.

"I don't have a family, Miss Professor."

"How horrible!" Emma exclaimed. "Doesn't the orphanage provide safe transportation for you?"

She stared at me and my friend as if trying to decide whether she should answer.

"No, ma'am. You needn't worry about me; I can take care of myself." There was an anxious tone in her voice, "Please excuse me, I really must be going now." She turned to go.

"Wait! I have something for you." I opened my purse and withdrew a tubular metal whistle on a chain. My grandfather had given it to me when, as a child, I had been obsessed with running races, another habit my mother thought was unladylike. I hated to part with it, but I hated still more the thought of harm befalling this sweet young girl.

"Put this around your neck," I said. "If you ever feel threatened, blow this whistle as loudly as you can. It will summon help and cause any bad people to flee."

She held the whistle in her small hand, blew a brief toot on it, and smiled. She put it around her neck and said, "Thank you, Miss Professor. You are very kind. May fortune smile upon you."

"You're most welcome," I said. "Now be careful."

"That poor thing," Emma said as the girl disappeared into the darkness. "To think the orphanage allows her to walk home by herself."

"My dear Emma, did you see her feet? And the clothes under her servant's smock are quite ragged. I fear she may be living on the street."

"Oh no! We must do something about it," Emma said. "We should not have allowed her out of our sight without ensuring she is not in danger."

"She's gone," I said, looking all around. "There's nothing to be done now. Let's be sure to speak to her again tomorrow."

When we returned to the exhibition hall, the ruckus had subsided. The maintenance crew had roped off the damaged stairway and the victims had been either tended to or taken to a hospital. O'Malley and Harrison were nearby, conversing with Mr. Wagstaffe about the incident.

"It's been an exhausting day," I said to O'Malley. "I have decided to return the hotel. Would you like to share a taxi with us?"

"Thank you, no, I'll be here a while longer," Tom replied.

As we departed I overheard Harrison saying, "If I were you, old chum, I wouldn't let that one get away."

I looked back to see both of them glancing my way.

⚙⚙⚙⚙⚙

Having retired early, the next morning found me eager to resume my duties as a judge. I had resolved to put the roguish Mr. Montague out of my mind and keep my focus upon my responsibilities as a judge. Enough of these silly schoolgirl antics, I told myself.

When Emma and I met O'Malley in the lobby of the hotel to share our usual cab ride, his eyes had puffy circles under them.

"Was it a late evening of interviews, Tom? At a pub perhaps?"

"Well, we started out investigating the incident, of course. We must have interviewed at least a dozen people apiece before the police cleared the place. After that, we decide to retire to the pub." He shook his head. "All those war stories and toasts, and 'let's have another round!'" I don't know how Harrison does it."

"I thought the Irish were supposed to be accomplished drinkers," Emma remarked.

His response was a frown, and I laughed in turn.

"You mentioned the incident," I said. "Did anyone determine what caused it?"

He shrugged. "The prevailing theory is that it was some sort of gas explosion on the mezzanine level. Though if I recall correctly, the area above was just an open balcony, so where were the gas lines situated?"

"Again, very curious," I replied.

O'Malley said nothing until the taxi arrived, this one a horse-drawn carriage that had been converted to steam power. "Crystal Palace," he told the driver. When we had taken our seats, he gave me a look of forced cheer. "Did you enjoy being a judge yesterday?" he asked.

"Definitely," I said. "And my duties are not over. There are 16 semi-finalists who must submit new dishes this morning. After that, I can actually spend the afternoon at my leisure. How about you?"

"I have a schedule full of interviews, thanks to Harrison, who has his contacts in these circles." He paused as if considering his words carefully. "I suppose you'll be spending your time with that foppish young man I saw you conversing with at the bookseller's stall."

"Foppish?" I raised my eyebrows and smiled. "Expensively dressed, yes, but certainly not excessively. And if I do choose to spend some time with him, what of it?"

"We know nothing about him. He may be a libertine."

"Surely you're not jealous, Mr. O'Malley," Emma grinned.

"Of course not! As a friend, I'm merely worried for your safety."

"Tom," I patted his arm to reassure him. "You have nothing to worry about. I am certainly old enough to judge a man's character for myself. But I do appreciate your concern. You're like the big brother I never had."

"Right," he nodded, exhaling a bit too loudly.

Emma and I exchanged glances. After we had parted company with Tom, she whispered to me, "Mr. O'Malley did not appreciate your last remark."

"But it is exactly how I feel," I said. "He is very dear to me."

"Oh, Ione." Emma smiled and squeezed my hand. "For such a bright girl, you can be rather dense at times."

"Drat!" I exclaimed, ignoring her remark. "I forgot to tell him about the potato man. I guess that will have to wait 'til later."

As luck would have it, I would be judging Montague once again in the first session of the morning. At least, that was what my program said, though when I arrived at the contest area, his was the only station that was presently unoccupied. All the other contestants were already well into their preparations. Whether or not O'Malley's suspicions about Montague were correct, punctuality was obviously not among the man's virtues.

"Professor Ione D?" A man in an elegant but dated suit took a seat next to me at the judges' table. "I am Damien Tuttle of the English Cook's Guild."

"Very pleased to meet you. I am most honored to..."

At that moment a tall wiry man wearing a derby and a monocle hurried up to claim the third on the other side of mine. "Professor!" he exclaimed, as he extended a hand for me to shake. "I am Edgar Fox of the Epicurean Society. I was delighted to hear you would be judging. I was opposed to bending the rules until I heard it would be you."

"Bend the rules?" Tuttle asked.

"I'm an American," I said. "One of the original judges met with an accident, so Mr. Wagstaffe invited me to be a substitute. It has been a great honor, and very enlightening."

"It's an honor of which you are most deserving."

"Thank you. I really hope we won't have any unpleasant incidents of the sort we had yesterday, with exploding contestants and showers of glass."

Mr. Fox leaned in closer and lowered her voice. "I heard from the Crystal Palace staff that the police have arrested two of those Irish malcontents who were here on opening day."

"Really?" Though I decided not to voice my suspicions, it didn't make sense for the Irish picketers to behave in such a heinous fashion if they meant to gain sympathy for their cause. "I was wondering if all these unfortunate events had been connected."

"You have a keen intellect, Professor D. There were two other suspects, who have apparently fled. However, the staff have all been alerted to their descriptions, so I believe we have nothing to worry about."

"Let us hope so," said Tuttle.

I was not surprised to see Emma in the audience, but this morning O'Malley and Harrison were both present as well. It was always a comfort to have Tom around, and I felt sad that he had taken exception to my likening him to a brother. He was always so kind and protective of me, and I loved him for that. His eyes met mine, and he gave me a warm smile. Harrison said something to him and both turned their eyes to the cooks' station.

Neville Montague arrived, with his sister in tow. The two of them spoke in hushed tones as they unpacked their supplies. At one point, he whispered something in his sister's ear, whereupon she gave me a curious look. I glanced at the other judges, both of whom were immersed in their notes and seemed to take no notice.

I reminded myself that I knew nothing of Neville Montague and his family situation. In my case, I was here to be a judge, not to encourage mysterious, roguish young men.

I am honored to serve as a judge in the final round
with Dame Leonora and Sir Phillip.
Illustration by Suzanne Stewart

Chapter 10. The Contest Continues

During this part of the contest, there was little for us to do but watch the chefs work. I noticed that Montague would occasionally look up at the judges' table. He was not like the other contestants, who would regard us with nervous glances. He seemed to be looking at me specifically. Such a rascal he was! I vowed to do my best to be impartial despite his impropriety.

As I watched the Montagues interact, I realized for the first time that Neville's sister was doing the lion's share of the work, while he occupied himself mainly with stirring and seasoning. Many of the other cooks were very controlling, leaving little for the assistants to do, but it was obvious that he trusted her.

At this round of the competition, all the entries were first rate, and I found it difficult to rank one over the other. Still, Montague's dish was once again the best. This time, he served a delectable roast pheasant with a delightful mushroom gravy. When we announced him as the winner, he remained composed with a smile and a bow. His sister, however, clapped and embraced him on hearing the news. My fellow judges frowned at her display of emotion, but I found her enthusiasm quite endearing.

I excused myself and joined Emma, who was waiting for me in the causeway. We would finally be able to spend an afternoon together. While touring the exhibits, we once again encountered the boorish potato chopper man. He was demonstrating his invention in a loud voice as it chugged along, peeling potatoes ten at a time. We gave him a wide berth, crossing to the other side of the promenade. Our encounters with the other vendors were pleasant enough. I took notes and sketched some of the devices. My students would find them fascinating.

At tea time we found a stall that reminded me of a tea-house we had frequented in our school days.

"These scones are excellent," I said, taking a demure bite.

"They certainly are," Emma replied. "My dear Ione, it's been so wonderful to have some time to reminisce, and talk about old friends, and perhaps some new ones."

"Yes, Emma, it's been lovely, despite your constant attempts to find me a husband."

Emma smiled and put her hand on my arm. "In all seriousness, I'm very proud of you and what you've accomplished. I hate to think that you have no one to share it with."

"Emma, I'm fine! I'm just not ready for that yet."

She laughed "I'd be remiss in my duty as your friend to help you find a good match. Don't forget, I single-handedly found husbands for both Marjorie and Louise."

"I know," I sighed.

Emma took a sip of tea and set the cup down. "Speaking of the Montague fellow – no, this is a different topic. Don't you think his reaction to winning was a little odd?"

"I'll admit it was rather subdued. But his sister was excited enough for the both of them."

"It's so fascinating to see all the chefs practicing their craft. One can certainly detect how the many years of experience have made their actions seem automatic. Neville Montague was a bit different. I couldn't help but notice that his sister was doing most of the work."

"Yes," I agreed. "Did you see how, when he was chopping mushrooms, she actually took the knife out of his hands and did it herself?"

"No," Emma replied, "I missed that. What do you think it means?"

"I think Mr. Montague is a fraud. As far as I could tell, his sister is the one who is really in charge. I suspect that he is not who he seems to be."

"Pish-tosh! How could he have made it all the way to the finals if he doesn't know what he's doing?" She laughed. "We seem to have switched roles. Weren't you just telling me I was being too suspicious?"

"Speaking of the finals," I said, "I wonder who the other contestants will be. As happy as I would be to see some new chefs get their chance, it would be very disappointing if MacTavish and Fenimore were not involved."

"I quite agree."

"It gives me butterflies in my stomach," Emma said. "What will happen next?"

❀❀❀❀❀

The contest finals were to be in the Concert Hall, an auditorium within the Crystal Palace with seating for over 4000 people. Since it was situated on the second floor, and the primary stairways had been destroyed, the management had erected a makeshift arrangement of wooden steps, with a canvas awning covering the open area above. At least a dozen of the tuxedo-clad guards were on duty to make sure there was no further mayhem.

The Hall was much like an opera house, with a tier of private boxes ringing the upper level. The box in the very center was reserved for the Royal Family and their guests. It was all the more exciting because I had inherited Mrs. White's position as a judge in the final round.

"It's unfortunate that we can't sit together," I told Emma.

"That's alright, dear, I'm sure there will be room in the press area. Right, Mr. O'Malley?"

"The Exhibition staff has set aside an entire row for the Press," he replied. "I'm sure there'll be room for you, Mrs. Farrington."

"An entire row? I don't think I shall need quite so much space."

We both giggled at Emma's joke. Tom sighed and shook his head.

The first thing I noticed upon entering was the clanks and clangs of pots and pans being set out. At center stage was a raised platform with four metal tables where the chefs' assistants were already at work. To the left, and raised two feet higher, was another platform with a table and chairs for the judges. Dame Leonora was there, seated next to a bearded gentleman wearing a deep blue vest, a long-sleeved white shirt, and a black top hat.

I parted ways with Tom and Emma and took my place in the third, unoccupied seat. After all that had transpired so far this week, I was surprisingly calm.

"My dear," Dame Leonora greeted me. "You look lovely this evening," She then introduced the man seated between us, Sir Phillip Cask of Domicile Books, a publisher of cookbooks and other domestically related titles. He was quite gracious, standing and kissing my hand as I arrived, though there was a strong odor of gin about him.

Opposite us, to the right of the chefs' area was a speaker's podium, which was currently unoccupied. In the orchestra pit in front of the stage were six chairs on which sat a number of youthful musicians holding various brass instruments. As the audience filed in, they began to play a stirring piece I recognized as Handel's Water Music.

After a while, the chamber music stopped, and a familiar anthem took its place: God Save the King. A voice from somewhere said, "His Majesty, King Edward the Seventh, by God's grace, Sovereign of the United Kingdom of Great Britain and Ireland, and Emperor of India." Everyone stood at once.

From my vantage point, I could clearly see the royal couple enter. It was quite exciting; in my time in London, I had never caught more than a glimpse of the late Queen Victoria. Her son and heir, King Edward, wore a smart ceremonial uniform. The Queen Princess wore an elegant formal gown. Once the royal party had entered their box, the anthem concluded and we all sat.

Professor Ione D. & the Epicurean Incident

A tall, well-dressed man with steel-gray hair ascended the steps to the podium. He raised a brass megaphone to his lips. "Good evening, ladies and gentlemen," he boomed. "I am Basil Huntington of the British Epicurean Society, and it is my pleasure to introduce you to our four finalists." As everyone had expected, MacTavish and Fenimore were among this group. The others were the young upstart Neville Montague and Agnes Richards of the Denton Culinary Academy. I was pleased to see that Miss Richards had made it into this select group.

Next, he introduced the judges. Each of us stood in turn to polite applause. He then gave a summary of the rules of the contest. As before, the judges would score each entry from 1 to 10 points. The difference was that the winner would receive his or her trophy from King Edward. In addition, His Majesty would sample each dish and award a Royal Medal of Merit to his favorite.

My mouth was very dry, so I took a long drink from the water glass in front of me. Sir Phillip took a sip from his own glass. By its potent smell, I could tell that it was not water.

The finalists and their assistants went to work. All wore white kitchen uniforms, except for MacTavish. Instead of pants, he wore a kilt decorated with his clan's tartan. His assistant was, of course, Angus, the mechanical man, wearing a matching kilt around his metal waist and a Union Jack on a pole attached to its back. The machine trundled back and forth around the table, doing most of the work in response to MacTavish's bellowed commands and wild gestures.

Fenimore, on the other hand, was filled with an energy that provided a sharp contrast to his unassuming appearance. He and his assistant Lang were furiously chopping vegetables. Though in my experience with cooking contests, such preparations are generally done beforehand, Fenimore's strategy made sense. His ingredients would be the freshest. Despite their furious activity, I noticed that the Chinaman occasionally cast an evil glare at MacTavish.

Just to be certain, I looked all around and was relieved to see no sign of the potato man.

Miss Richards was clearly in charge of her station. Her assistant was a slight man, as meek and self-effacing as she was imposing. She did most of the work and seemed to rely on him as an afterthought.

Montague appeared to be the calmest of the four contestants, looking frequently to the audience as if relishing the attention of the ladies in the front row. His sister was once again the driving force on their entry, and she worked with a stoic efficiency.

Though watching the chefs working was fascinating, I was also interested to see the journalists at work. Tom and Harrison took notes with utmost seriousness. Most of the reporters seemed to be mainly watching Fenimore and MacTavish, who were located toward the left side of the stage. It made me feel quite sympathetic to Montague and Richards. Something in me hoped one of them would win, and put the glory hounds in their place.

The chefs had additional help. The youthful servers from the previous night scurried about like busy chipmunks, collecting garbage and dirty pots and pans. I was relieved to see that the little Chinese girl Lily was among them. Emma waved to her from the press area, but if the girl noticed, she was too busy to respond.

To entertain the audience while the chefs worked, the ensemble played several numbers. While this was happening, Sir Phillip leaned towards me and said, "I have read your book. It was quite fascinating, though I would take issue with the chapter on parboiling. If one takes care to minimize the amount of water one uses, it does not necessarily have an adverse effect on the flavor of the dish."

"Is that so?" I replied. Sir Phillip was a pleasant enough fellow if one could ignore the overpowering smell of gin on his breath. "I beg your pardon. I believe this would be a good time to stretch our limbs. We have a long night of judging ahead of us."

"You are quite right," he said. "Please do. Exercise is most healthful for the constitution." As I got up from my chair, I noted that he took the opportunity to use his elbow muscles to have another nip from his flask.

I noticed Emma look up from her notes and give me a smile. She was playing the part of reporter dutifully, jotting down notes on her program. I dearly wished I could sit with her, but decided instead to stand for a while at the other end of the judge's table.

"Dame Leonora," I said to the diminutive lady, "I want to say once again what an honor this is to be chosen for this panel. I feel humbled by the presence of such luminaries."

"Nonsense, dear, we are very glad to have you."

"Thank you very much," I said. "This has always been a dream of mine."

"Speaking of that," Leonora said, "I had the most peculiar dream last night. The dinosaur statues came to life and broke through the walls of the Palace. They went on quite a rampage." She laughed. "Silly me, it was probably the excitement from the gas explosion and all."

"At least we needn't worry about that," I smiled, "Since they are long extinct."

"Ladies and gentlemen!" A loud voice interrupted us. It was Wagstaffe, now standing behind the potion, speaking into the trumpet-like device. "As we have some time before the entries are ready for judging, please allow me to say a few words about the Epicurean Society, our history and mission."

"Oh goodness," chuckled Leonora. "Mr. Wags is a dear but he can go on for quite some time. I suppose we should take our places and at least pretend to listen."

"I suppose," I nodded, disappointed that I would not get to speak to her a while longer. I walked back across the podium to take my seat.

It seemed like hours, though my pocket watch indicated only twenty minutes before Wagstaffe finished speaking and took his seat. The ensemble resumed playing and treated us to some wonderful selections by Mozart and Haydn. As time passed, the delicious aroma of cooking filled the auditorium. In the past few days, I had sampled over a dozen examples of first-rate cuisine, yet I could hardly wait to try the products of these very talented chefs.

While Wagstaffe spoke, I noticed O'Malley making sketches on a large artist's pad. I knew from personal experience that he was quite talented. At one point he tore off a page and handed it to Emma, who smiled and looked up at me.

Chef MacTavish struggles to get Angus to deliver the
food to the judges.
Illustration by José Cardeñas

Chapter 11. The Four Finalists

When Lord Huntington rose from his seat, I knew our wait was almost over. "Ladies and gentleman," he announced. "Please take your seats. The dishes are now finished and ready to be judged. Note that for this final round there will be a fourth judge, King Edward himself."

At the name of the sovereign, the audience broke into spontaneous applause. Huntington held up a hand to silence the crowd.

"His Majesty shall be sampling each of the four dishes and making his own selection. The King's Trophy is a separate award from the Gold Medal of the Epicurean Society, so it is quite possible that there will be not one but two winners tonight."

"Now, I will call the name of each contestant in random order. As I call each name, the chef will dish out four portions of each recipe. The assistant must distribute these to the three judges as the chef personally brings the last portion to His Majesty."

I looked up into the stands to the Royal Box. I could just barely see the King's bearded face gazing down at the rest of us. Beside him sat his wife, Queen Alexandra, and a contingent of royal guards.

Just as it seemed all was going well, there was yet another disturbance. Three couples who had been sitting only three rows from the stage suddenly stood up, linked arms, and began singing, "The Wearin' O' the Green." A disapproving murmur arose from the audience.

"What's this, then?" Sir Philip roared in anger. He sprang to his feet, causing his half-empty glass of gin to wobble dangerously. "Get those bloody Irish out of here!"

"My goodness, what next?" I remarked to no one in particular. The uniformed guards rushed quickly from the sidelines to remove the protesters. It was a reminder that, popular as he was, the British monarch was not universally loved.

"Our first finalist," boomed Huntington, "is Professor Agnes Richards of the Denton Culinary Academy. Her dish is roast pheasant with potatoes and herbs." The audience responded with a smattering of polite applause. Miss Richards placed the plate onto a tray with a domed cover to keep the food warm and headed up the stairs to His Majesty's box. Her elderly assistant bore a larger tray to the judges' platform and set a dish in front of each of us with somber efficiency.

I raised my fork and took a delicate mouthful. After

having tried so many complex and sophisticated dishes over the past two days, I had expected the experience to be anticlimactic. That was not the case. The potatoes were roasted to a soft, creamy perfection, while the pheasant had none of the gamy flavor that wild bird sometimes had. It was more than just the judicious use of spices. This fowl tasted like it been raised domestically and fed nothing but prime grains. Furthermore, I could tell it had been aged to a tender perfection. I recorded my observations in my notebook, knowing that the next might be just as impressive.

"Mr. Neville Montague of the Conqueror's Tavern in Brighton; a whitefish poached in wine on a bed of asparagus and white rice." Again there was polite applause. Once again the assistant, in this case, Neville's sister, served us. When I glanced his way, Montague gave me a brief nod of recognition, which I declined to return.

I was quite anxious to taste his offering. His earlier dishes had reflected considerable boldness, but did he have the skills to match his attitude? My face must have betrayed my skepticism because Neville's sister had lingered half a moment to give me a hopeful smile. Young Lily, followed behind her with a water pitcher to refill our glasses.

The fragrance of the dish told me that my doubts about Montague were wrong. This was a recipe that could rival even my mother's heavenly bouillabaisse. The meat of the fish was tender and flaky; the sauce subtle and complex. The rice was superb, light and fluffy without a hint of stickiness. It made me wonder what the next entry would have in store. I looked toward the chef's table and saw that Montague had already returned from the Royal Box. He met my gaze and smiled. His sister tapped him on the shoulder and gave him a reproachful look, upon which he joined her in cleaning up.

"And our third dish," Huntington announced, "Is by Sir Charles Fenimore, a Cornish style chowder with freshly baked bread. A daring choice of modest fare, yet Sir Charles is widely respected for his elevation of working class dishes to culinary perfection." At the mention of Fenimore's name, the crowd's reaction became more enthusiastic; there were cheers in addition to the clapping.

I had not, until this point, paid much notice to Fenimore's assistant Lang Min. As he set the dish in front of each of us, he gave a gracious bow of the head but when he reached me, he avoided my gaze. I realized why Emma had found him to be disagreeable.

I looked back toward the chef's tables. Fenimore was just returning from his trek up the stairs to the Royal Box. He seemed completely unruffled with his encounter with the King. His expression was aloof, almost bored, as he awaited the judges' decision.

Perhaps my expectations for Sir Fenimore had been too high. The chowder was very good, a hearty meal that would be especially welcome in cold weather. Maybe this was what had propelled his cooking to such popularity. However, I thought it a lackluster choice for such an illustrious contest.

"Lastly," called Lord Huntington, "We have Mr. Magnus MacTavish..." The moment he mentioned the name, two dozen kilt-clad highlanders sitting in the highest part of the auditorium stood up and cheered.

"Quiet, please!" the announcer scolded. "Anyone causing a disturbance shall be asked to leave the auditorium." The rowdy bunch fell silent, and Huntington continued, "Mr. MacTavish is serving a curried Scottish lamb, accompanied by sautéed vegetables and finely diced fruit. He is known for surpassing the boundaries of culinary tradition, in that his dishes incorporate elements of the cuisine of many far-flung parts of the Empire."

In truth, all the dishes so far had been exquisite. It would be exceedingly difficult to pick one over all the rest. But it was MacTavish's offering that I anticipated the most – not so much because of the man's reputation but because I craved a more robust alternative to the generally tame flavors of the food I'd sampled so far.

I leaned to one side to get a better look at MacTavish at his station. Although this evening's protocol held that the food was to be served by the cook's assistant, his helper was by no means ordinary. Even so, he surprised me once again. Unlike the other chefs, who had modestly kept their silence, he turned in our direction and spoke.

"Ladies and gents of the judging panel," MacTavish proclaimed, "Your Highness," he looked toward the monarch and bowed, "Prepare yer taste buds to be amazed and astonished. Angus," he commanded the automaton, "Serve the food." Angus extended its left arm and picked up a large circular tray, which it balanced easily on the flat surface of that appendage. With the other arm, it picked up the plates one at a time and placed them neatly on the tray. It then turned toward the judges' table and headed our way, gears whirring and wheels squeaking.

I expected that like the other contestants, MacTavish would bring the food to the King while his assistant served us. The problem was that Angus had wheels instead of feet, which would not be able to climb the stairs to the judges' platform, but MacTavish had a solution.

As the mechanical man trundled toward us, the chef preceded his creation with something that looked like a rolled up carpet. When MacTavish reached the stairs he placed one end on the platform – which somehow attached itself to the wooden floor – and walked back, unrolling a rigid flat surface which he fastened to the floor of the stage. He watched as Angus reached the makeshift ramp and started to ascend, then he returned to his station to get the portion that was to go to King Edward.

Once on the platform, Angus stopped in front of Dame Leonora and swiveled around on its base. It raised its free arm and grasped one of the plates by its edge, using the clamp at the end of that limb. Leonora moved back reflexively as the shiny metal arm swung rapidly in her direction, but it stopped just short of her face. The audience gave a collective gasp, with scattered bursts of laughter.

MacTavish had just begun to ascend the stairs when he heard the crowd's reaction. "No, no, no!" he cried. "Serve the food, I order ye!" He set the tray down at his station and stormed over to where the automaton was standing.

At that moment, Angus came back to life. With a slow, gentle motion it set the plate down on the table in front of Leonora. The titters of the crowd gave way to applause. The judge leaned forward to savor its fragrance. She looked about the plate for the fresh utensils which were normally provided, then smiled when she realized MacTavish had defied protocol again. "Chopsticks," she said as she picked up the wooden sticks, a bemused look on her face.

"What did I tell ye, folks?" MacTavish cried. "Old Angus just needs some encouragement now and then." He turned, went back the chef's table, grabbed the tray, and again started up the stairs.

Angus rolled forward once more and stopped in front of Sir Phillip. Again it raised its free arm and grabbed the plate, which it swung out in the judge's direction. This time it stopped suddenly with the plate suspended in the air halfway to its destination.

"What bloody foolishness!" Sir Phillip exclaimed. "It may be fine as a glorified onion chopper, but it makes a simply atrocious waiter." He stood up from his chair and reached over to take the plate, knocking over his glass of gin in the process.

"No! Wait!" MacTavish, clearly agitated, bounded down the stairs with the king's tray still in his hand. He set it down at the chef's station, picked up a screwdriver, and hurried up the ramp to our table. "Ye've got to follow the proper procedure. All Angus needs is a wee bit of tinkering." He opened the automaton's access panel on the side and adjusted something within. For a moment, nothing happened, then with a hiss it emitted a cloud of steam from its bulb-shaped head. A stream of oil dribbled to the floor.

"C'mon, ye rusted bucket of bolts," the Scotsman muttered. "Deliver the food or it's to the scrapheap with ye!" The audience responded with laughter.

As if it had comprehended its owner's threat, the gears inside of it began whirring once again. Its arm resumed its motion and lay the plate in front of Sir Phillip, then it turned to roll forward in my direction, at half its previous speed. Its motions were now so jerky, the plate on the tray it carried almost spilled. Nevertheless, the Scottish contingent rose to cheer.

"Ladies and gentleman," scolded Lord Huntington. "Let me remind you that we will have no more such outbursts. And Mr. MacTavish, pray continue. We must not keep His Majesty waiting." He gestured toward the Royal Box.

I glanced down at Emma, seated in the front row with the press, laughing at MacTavish's follies. From a spectator's viewpoint, she found amusement in this insanity. For the sake of the good people of the Epicurean Society, however, I hoped the troubles were over.

My prayers were unanswered. For the third time, the mechanical man turned to face the table and moved its right arm to grasp the plate on the tray. Once again it bore the plate in the correct direction, and once again it stopped halfway to its destination.

A hush fell over the audience. Aside from a few titters of laughter, it seemed that everyone else in the auditorium was looking at MacTavish to see how he would respond.

"Why you..." His face went red and he clenched his fist. "I ought to... I've got half a mind to..." He turned to the audience. "Just another teeny difficulty," he said. There was a look of frustration on his face as he turned and walked back toward his creation.

"Mr. MacTavish, please, we've had our fill of your tomfoolery," boomed Lord Huntington. "Kindly deliver the tray to His Majesty."

"But... the last plate." stammered MacTavish.

"The serving girl can handle it. Young lady," he addressed Lily, who had been refilling our water glasses. "Take the last plate from the automaton and serve it to Professor D."

Lily set her pitcher down on the table next to me. Because Angus was the same height as a tall man, the diminutive girl had to stand on her tip toes to reach the plate. She managed to get hold of it, then, as she pulled it down, a look of alarm came over her face. She sniffed at the food, frowning.

"Is something the matter, dear?" I asked. She continued staring at it, wrinkling her nose. To me, the smell of the curry was mouth-watering, though Lily seemed to find it troubling.

"Young lady," Huntington called from the podium, "What is the delay?"

"Do as you're told, girl," Sir Phillip said as he struggled with his chopsticks, managing to take a few small bites. "Can't let the food get cold; it's simply delicious." He turned away and muttered, "As for these blasted Chinese utensils, however..."

Lily's dark eyes seemed to implore me for direction. Then she closed her eyes and released the plate. She grimaced and jumped back as it hit the floor, shattering and spattering chunks of lamb and yellow curry everywhere.

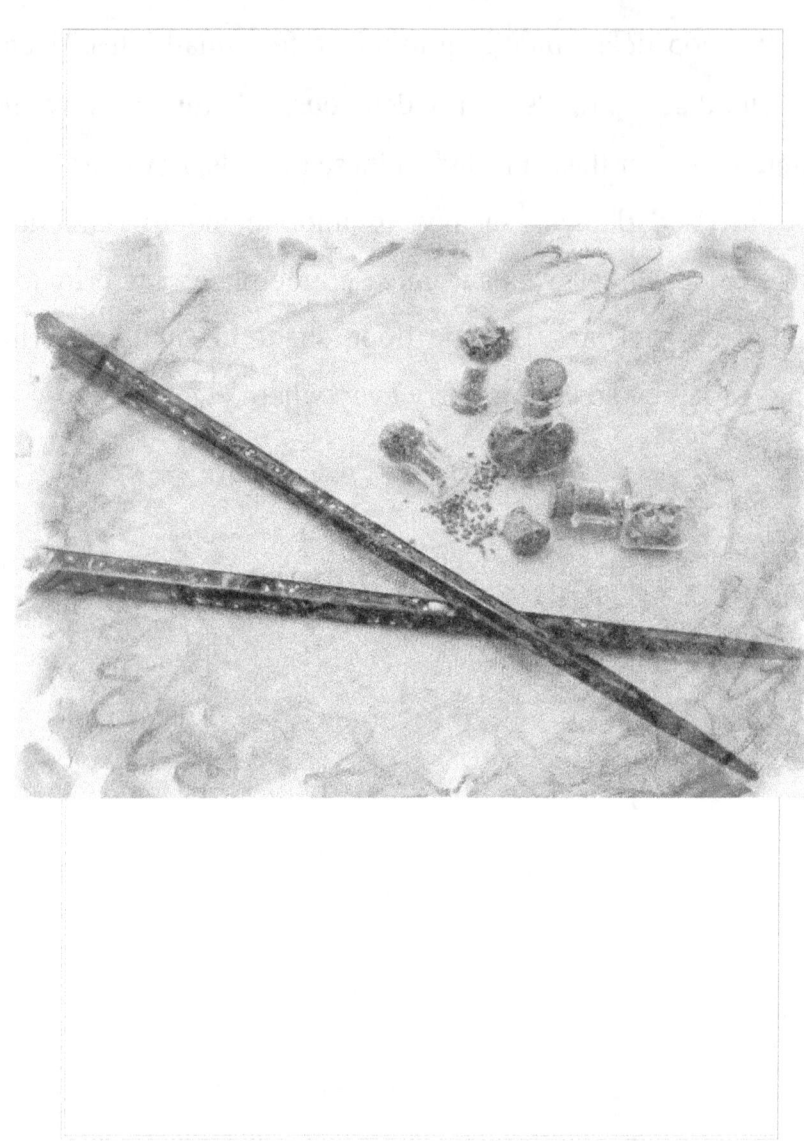

Could it have been the chopsticks?
Illustration by Arlys Holloway

Chapter 12. MacTavish's Mess

"Good heavens!" I cried, jumping back instinctively, causing my chair to make a loud scrape on the platform. Lily backed away and stood at the edge, looking from one direction to the other in panic. From the crowd came shouts of surprise and indignation.

"Why you little yellow devil!" The kitchen matron charged over from the sidelines but found herself blocked by Mr. Wagstaffe and two other Society officials who stood there arguing among themselves. Undeterred, she pushed her way through. "Clean up this mess at once, girl, or I'll see you on the next boat back to China!"

"No!" Lily took shelter behind the stationary Angus. "Don't eat it!" she cried to the other two judges. "Don't touch it! It's poisoned!"

"Poison!" came a cry from the crowd.

"The Scotsman tried to poison the king!" The auditorium exploded in a tumult of voices.

MacTavish leaped onto the judge's platform and shouted above the clamor. "This is outrageous slander! There is nothing wrong with my food. I would never, knowingly or unknowingly, harm His Majesty, or anybody else. Whoever says this is a bloody liar and I'll punch him in the face!"

Just then, Sir Phillip stood up, turned as if to go. He wobbled for a moment, then fell to his knees on the wooden platform and began vomiting off the edge.

"Good gracious, what now?" I sighed. Was the food really tainted, or was there another reason for the man's illness? I'd seen him consume half a glass of gin in one swallow

"Sir Phillip!" cried Leonora as she sprang to her feet. "Someone please call a doctor!" Her hands flew up to clutch her throat. She made gagging sounds, then swooned and fell with a thump. There were screams and cries from the audience. I stepped around the retching Sir Phillip to see if I could help her, but a crowd of officials and journalists had already surrounded her.

"Everyone, we must remain calm!" Huntington cried. "Stand back and give the judges some air!" His deep voice boomed over the chattering crowd. "Wagstaffe, summon a medical team at once!"

I turned back to the hapless Sir Philip, who now lay motionless on the floor. Before I could assist him, I heard Lily yelp in distress.

The kitchen matron, her face red with fury, had circled around from behind and grabbed hold of the poor girl's ear.

"Have you gone mad? I'll tan your hide, you worthless little twit!"

"Ow!" Lily struggled as the woman tried to drag her away. "Don't touch the food. Don't touch anything!"

"Madam, release her at once!" I cried.

"This is none of your concern, Yank. This cursed little monkey has embarrassed me for the last time!"

With the matron momentarily distracted, Lily wriggled free and hid behind my skirts.

"Lily, look at me," I said, pulling her around front. "Do you know who did this?"

Lily shook her head, sobbing loudly.

"Wouldn't surprise me if she did it herself," the matron growled. "Lassie, you are dismissed. Get out! I never want to see your squinty-eyed face 'round here again."

I was so angry I could scarcely speak. "Leave us!" I snapped at her.

With a huff, the horrible woman stormed off, almost colliding with a crew of orderlies rushed in with stretchers.

A man in formal attire stormed onto the stage. I recognized him as the doctor who had helped the victim of the burner explosion. "Take them to the infirmary, quicks," he ordered. The medics loaded first Leonora and then Phillip onto the stretchers.

Meanwhile, an angry mob was closing around MacTavish. Defiant, he continued to rant, "This is a plot against me! Someone has tainted my food to ruin my reputation!"

"Attention!" Huntington shouted, barely audible over the pandemonium. "Please, may I have your attention?"

At that moment Lily pulled the whistle I had given her from out of her shirt. She raised it to her lips and gave an ear-piercing blast. The crowd fell silent and everyone looked toward the sound. "Don't touch the chopsticks!" she cried. "Don't touch anything!"

"Ladies and gentlemen," Huntington commanded, "Please sit down and remain calm. Kindly wait for our ushers to escort you out of the hall in an orderly fashion. To all of you, we make our deepest apologies for this most unfortunate incident."

"Is His Majesty safe?" someone shouted.

"Rest assured," Huntington responded, "That His and Her Majesties are safe and have departed."

Lily turned as if to run away. I grabbed her by the shoulder. She buried her face in my blouse, sobbing. "Lily, talk to me!"

"Ione, are you alright?" Somehow Tom had made his way through the frantic throngs of people, followed by Emma.

"Goodness, what a mess!" Emma narrowly missed stepping in the spilled food as she joined us, her handkerchief over her mouth to filter out the pungent smell.

"Yes, I'm fine," I said. "Though I can't say the same for the other judges."

"Young lady, can you tell me what happened?" Tom asked Lily. "Was it poison?"

"Yes," She said. "In the curry. It was *fu zi*; I recognized the scent."

"Foo what?" Tom asked.

"I've heard of that," I said. "A Chinese herb, I believe."

"But how can it be poison?" Emma countered. "I was watching Dame Leonora, and I did not see her take a single bite."

"Really?" I said. "Why then did she collapse?"

"I wonder if she had some other medical condition," Tom speculated. "Or was it something besides the food?" he bent down to examine the mess on the floor of the platform.

"Please, please don't touch it!" cried Lily.

"Of course!" I cried, stepping back with my heart pounding.

"What?" Emma asked.

"Certain substances that can be absorbed through the skin," I explained.

"The chopsticks!" Emma and I spoke the words together.

"The chopsticks?" asked Tom.

"The chopsticks," Lily nodded through her tears.

"Let's consider what we know," I said, lowering my voice. "Surely MacTavish wouldn't poison his own cooking. Lily, did you see anyone tampering with the food? The police will need to know."

She shook her head.

"The gloves!" Emma cried. "That Ling Min fellow was wearing gloves!"

"Could he be the culprit?" I asked.

MacTavish's voice rose above the din of the crowd. "Fenimore you bastard!" he shouted, shaking his fist, "You did this to me!"

"That accusation is ludicrous," Fenimore shouted back.

"I'll go speak to the police," Tom said. "Stay here, Ione, where you'll be safe."

"Yes, Tom," I said, too excited by the situation to be annoyed at him.

"Attention, everyone!" A uniformed man strode to the podium and addressed the crowd in a booming voice. "I am Superintendent St. James of the Metropolitan Police. Thank you for your patience. Those persons involved in the contest must remain in this room until I have given them leave. The rest of you must exit the auditorium immediately."

"This is quite serious," I said. "Lily, you saved my life!" I bent down, putting my hands on her shoulders. "Tell me, what did you smell?"

Before she could answer, Harrison pushed past us to the police commander, with O'Malley following close behind him. "Superintendent St. James! Sir, can you tell us what's going on? Is this a case of poisoning? Could it have been an assassination attempt?"

"It's too soon to comment on the possibility of food poisoning or anything else, as the doctors are currently attending to the victims. As for your second question, we have no knowledge of any threats or attempts on His Majesty's life."

The police captain turned to one of his men. "Sergeant Sanders, go to the kitchens and remain there to make sure none of the staff leaves until we've had a chance to question them. Furthermore, make sure that nothing is removed from the kitchen. Make sure they wash nothing! Now, where is the girl who started all this chaos?"

Lily's big brown eyes went wide with fear. "It wasn't me!"

"Lily, it's alright." To the Captain, I said, "Sir, I am responsible for her."

"Good," St. James replied. "Do not allow her to leave; she is a witness."

He went to join his underlings who were now examining the automaton. I could hear the loud bickering of MacTavish and Fenimore.

"Silence, both of you!" roared the captain.

I took the distraught girl by the hand to comfort her. Big tears rolled down her face.

"Here, dear." Emma reached into her purse and pulled out a lace handkerchief, which she used to dab the tears from Lily's face before handing it to her. To me, she said, "When I asked Nigel to accompany me here, he said it would be a colossal bore. He'll have to eat his words now, won't he?"

"Indeed," I replied. "Now Lily, what exactly is this fu zi? How did you know about it?"

"From the smell," Lily sniffled. "I knew something was wrong, but there were so many scents. At first, I thought it was the curry. The spiciness was burning my eyes."

Emma squatted down to speak to her on her level. "If you thought it was poisoned, dear, why didn't you tell someone?"

"I didn't know until I smelled it up close. Then I remembered Madame Chang, who worked at the orphanage in Hong Kong. She taught me about Chinese medicine. 'The nose is the herbalist's most important tool,' she would say."

"I'm afraid my nose failed the test," I said, "All I could smell was curry."

"But this fu zi," Emma said, "Are you saying it's poison?"

"I remember now why this word sounded familiar," I said. "I've read about this plant. We call it wolfsbane or monks hood. It can be quite dangerous."

Lily nodded. "It is very powerful medicine and must be used only by those with great skill. Too much is deadly."

"There she is!" MacTavish pointed at Lily as he approached with a policeman following closely behind. "There is the girl who ruined my entry. Somebody must have put her up to it! That rat Fenimore!"

Lily gave her head a vigorous shake. "No, sir, I didn't! I swear it!"

Emma stood in front of her protectively. "This girl is a heroine. She saved Professor D. from being poisoned."

"This is not an accusation," said the policeman. "We'll need you to answer a few questions, young lady." Lily tried to hide behind Emma, but he grabbed the girl by the arm.

"Is this really necessary?" Emma objected.

"Yes!" replied the officer. "Madam, please do not interfere."

Emma shot him a poisonous look. "Let me accompany her then!"

"No!" the policeman declared. For once, Emma was speechless.

"It will be fine, Lily," I said to her. "They only want to ask you questions. Tell them the truth. You did nothing wrong."

Lily shot back a frightened glance as the man led her away.

"The poor girl!" I remarked. "What a mess this has been!"

"I still don't understand why anyone would want to poison Dame Leonora," Emma said.

"Ma'am," interrupted a policeman with an inspector's insignia on his uniform. "If you're not involved in the contest, you need to be on your way."

Emma's face was stern and serious. "I'm with the press." She held up a piece of paper with the word 'Journalist' printed on it.

"Really? What publication, do you represent, madam?"

"I'm from the Ladies' Garden Society of Bolton. Um, the *Bulletin*."

"Then where is your notebook? I've never seen a reporter without one."

"I have an excellent memory."

The officer raised an eyebrow. "Very well, then." He raised his voice and addressed the press, shooting a pointed glance at Emma. "All reporters need to kindly refrain from interfering with the questioning of witnesses."

"Constable Smith!" He called to a nearby colleague.

"Sir?" This policeman was a tall, broad-shouldered young man with wavy blond hair.

"Escort the ladies to the audience area a few rows up." The inspector gave us a condescending look over his spectacles. "No need to subject them to this unpleasantness."

"Yes, sir. Ladies, please follow me."

"Thank you," I said, as he took us up to the seats, about ten rows back. I gave him a smile, though inside I was seething. Did the Superintendent think we would faint if we heard talk of plots and poisoning? If he only knew of all my adventures so far!

"Constable Smith, eh?" said Emma as she jotted his name down on her program, a hint of a smile on her face. "I think he fancies you. Police work may not be glamorous, but it's a very respectable occupation. I need to research his family. Did you catch his given name?"

"Emma, please!" I said. "This is neither the time nor the place for this. The judges appear to have been poisoned, poor little Lily is in trouble, and this exposition has become a disaster. And really, the Bolton Bulletin?"

"That's a real newsletter, and I do write a column for it. I'll have you know that my article on natural aphid repellent was well received and even posted at the counter of our local nursery."

"Emma," I said, trying to get her back on track, "You were seated near the cooking area. Did you observe anything suspicious while MacTavish and his... assistant were cooking? Did any of the servers tarry a bit too long by the table? Did you notice any strangers?"

She shook her head. "You don't think Lily had a hand in it, do you?"

"No, I do not."

"Unfortunately, other than young Lily," Emma said, "I hardly noticed how many other helpers there were, much less whether they seemed to belong here."

"There were three other children besides Lily. But I did not observe anything unusual in their behavior. No, if someone tainted the food, the best place to do it would have been in the kitchens. Someone could have substituted the *fu zi* herb for the real ingredients."

"That's a clever deduction, Ione."

I opened my purse and withdrew a pad and pencil. "I believe we need to start thinking like detectives."

At that, Emma's eyes brightened.

"I have an extra notebook if you'd like to jot down notes for your bulletin."

"You always come prepared," she smiled as I handed her the notebook.

A handsome young bobbie summons me for questioning
about the tragic incident.
Illustration by José Cardeñas

Chapter 13. An Impromptu Investigation

The popular idea of a crime scene is a romantic one of drama and intrigue, but that is not the case. It was tedious to watch the police question each of the chefs in turn. I checked my pocket watch; it was now well past midnight.

Since the excitement had worn off I now found myself becoming rather weary. The kitchen staff had brought up a large pot of coffee. By the time I'd noticed its arrival it was empty. This was unfortunate because I would have been willing to "sell my Aunt Fanny for a cup," as my father liked to say.

Emma attempted to save me from dozing off by engaging me in conversation, but I was not feeling very talkative. Instead I indulged in a favorite pastime from my youth: sketching the people and places around me.

"Your skill has really improved," my friend said, gazing over my shoulder.

"Tom has taught me many things about shading and perspective," I explained.

"That's a very humorous likeness of MacTavish," she giggled, but only for a moment. "It's a tragedy that so much went wrong with this Exhibition. The perpetrators and picketers ought to be arrested and charged with creating a national embarrassment. It reflects very poorly on His Majesty, for heaven's sake."

"I suspect that there may be more at play here than simple rabble rousing," I replied. "Nor do the organizers of the event seem to have been negligent. This may be the work of someone with an ax to grind."

"But who? Those Irish ne'er-do-wells? They seem to be quite peaceful. We've seen more violence between the chefs than from the protesters."

"How true," I laughed. "At least they're acting civil at the moment, and seem to be cooperating with the police questioning. I wish I could hear what they're saying."

It was that moment that we heard MacTavish explode yet again. "Are ye insinuating that I would poison my own cooking and ruin my reputation? Are you daft? Ha! That is what Fenimore would like you to believe."

"You cur!" shouted Fenimore from the press area where he was waiting. "You will be held accountable for that vile slander."

"That is enough, both of you," snapped St. James. "We are not accusing either one of you. We simply wish to look at this incident from every angle."

"I bloody well hope so!" MacTavish cried. "And the only angle is the point on that scalawag Fenimore's head. Tell me again why I would poison my own cooking."

"Why would I accuse you of malice when incompetence will do?" Fenimore's usually calm voice was charged with emotion. "No wonder your food is tainted, with that mechanized meat tenderizer spewing oil everywhere. Anyone who eats your food is being poisoned."

"Sir Fenimore," snapped the sergeant. "We are interviewing Mr. MacTavish at the moment. Kindly sit down, hold your tongue, and let us do our jobs."

"Quite right," echoed St. James. "We don't barge into your kitchen and tell you to put more salt on the roast beef, do we?"

"Professor Diff..." said a deep male voice from my right. I was startled to see the same young bobbie who had escorted us up to our seats.

"You may address me as Professor D," I said.

"Fine. Could you come with me then, Professor D?"

I rose to follow him and turned back to my friend. "I'll be right back, Emma."

She nodded and gave me a conspiratorial wink. "Keep an eye out for Lily."

"Of course."

The policeman led me down to the stage area, where Wagstaffe was anxiously trying to calm the still-furious MacTavish.

"Can you keep civil, or do we have to take you down to the station in handcuffs?" thundered Superintendent St. James. When he turned back to me, he was all smiles. "I'm sorry, miss, for all this unpleasantness, and keeping you here so late."

"I quite understand sir. Tell me, is there any word about the other judges, are they alright?"

St. James grimaced. "Not very well, I'm afraid. It does appear to have been poisoning, but at the moment, we have no idea about what it might be."

"Have you spoken with Lily? I believe she knows what the poison was."

"But of course. The girl was babbling something about somebody called Fu Zi. Since we know of no such person at the Exhibition, we concluded she was hysterical."

"*Sacre bleu,*" I muttered under my breath. "Superintendent, *fu zi* is not a person, it's a Chinese herb that has toxic properties."

The policeman sighed, shook his head and called for one of his men. "Collins, was it you that questioned the Chinese girl?"

"Yes, sir."

"I have further questions. Go fetch her at once."

"Sir!" The man nodded in acknowledgment and was on his way.

"Thank you, Professor. We are finished for the moment but do not leave the area."

"I won't." I returned to my seat next to Emma.

"Did you discover anything new?" my friend asked.

"No. I got the impression that we know more than they do. They thought 'fu zi' was a person, and concluded that Lily was hysterical."

"Did you see her?" Emma asked. "Why would they call her hysterical? Is she alright?"

I shrugged. "Men!"

"The police talked to Miss Richards for quite some time," she continued.

"That's curious." I looked toward the chef's area and noticed Agnes Richards sitting by herself, looking somber. "How unfortunate for her."

"Why?" Emma looked surprised. "You don't believe they suspect her, do you?"

"No, I don't. Her entry was the best of the evening, and she might well have won. This poisoning has robbed her of an important opportunity for her career."

"It was better than Montague's? From where I was sitting his dish smelled heavenly."

"Yes his was good, but... something's amiss," I said. "His behavior has been quite odd through this entire exhibition."

"I don't know about that," Emma replied. "In my experience, chefs can be very eccentric people." Her face brightened. "Look! The sergeant is speaking with him right now. I can't imagine he had anything to do with it. Criminals are never that handsome."

"I didn't say he was the culprit. I can't imagine what his motivation would be."

"Well, at the moment he appears to be motivated to speak to you."

I was surprised to see Neville approaching with his sister beside him. It had been a very short interrogation.

"Professor Dfrdwy," he said, "I've – we've – been quite concerned about you. Are you feeling any ill effects?"

"Thank you," I replied. "And no, I didn't taste the food, nor did I touch it." I looked at his sister. "I don't believe we have been introduced."

"Oh, how negligent of me. Professor, this is my sister, Nelda."

"Pleased to meet you, Miss Montague. This is my friend, Mrs. Emma Farrington."

"Charmed," Emma said. The two shook hands. "I was quite impressed by your hard work in the contest. What a tragedy that it's been cut short by this terrible incident."

Nelda smiled, "There should be considerable publicity for the family business. That will please Father greatly." She glanced at her brother and scowled.

Neville seemed not to notice. "I recall, Professor D, that you declined my earlier dinner invitation because I was still a contestant. As the contest has now been canceled, I would like to extend that invitation once more."

"That is very kind, Mr. Montague, but after all this, I have no appetite. Please excuse me, but it looks as if Miss Richards is preparing to depart. I would like a quick word with her."

"Oh, certainly," Neville said, his handsome face marred by a frown.

"Come along, Emma," I said. "You may want to take notes for your newsletter."

"Please excuse us, Mr. Montague, Miss Montague," Emma said.

As we approached, Richards was putting on her coat. Her assistant stood nearby, waiting patiently.

"Miss Richards," I said, "I am Professor Ione D of Gallard College in America. I just wanted to say how impressive your entry was."

"Why thank you," she said, looking a bit startled. "It's an honor to meet you. I'm halfway through your book, and it's fascinating. It's ironic that a book that captures the British character so well would be written by an American."

"Thank you," I replied. I was about to ask her how she had made her pheasant taste so savory, when she posed a question of her own.

"If you don't mind my asking," she said. "How did you manage to get a spot on the panel?"

"Agnes," her elderly assistant scolded, "That was rather a rude question."

Miss Richards glanced back at him. "Professor, this is my father, William Richards. And Da, I was not implying she was not fully qualified, but rather an outsider."

Emma hastened to defend me. "Professor Dfrdwy is not an outsider. She attended the same school as I did. Her parents were attached to the American Embassy here."

I related the story about Mrs. White's unfortunate accident. "I am merely a last-minute replacement by the Epicurean Society."

Agnes laughed. "Oh, I see. I hadn't heard." She sighed. "I was looking forward to speaking with Dame Leonora afterward. She has been an inspiration for me. I sincerely hope she makes a speedy recovery."

"As do I."

"Ah, Professor," said the young police officer as he approached us. "I've been looking all over for you. Would you kindly follow me?"

"Don't you want to question me?" Emma asked.

"For now, just Professor D.," he replied.

"Oh, piffle," she muttered as I followed him away.

The police had set up a few chairs in the upstage area past the judge's platform. The same officer who had chased Emma and me away was there waiting for me.

"Professor D.," he said, "I am Inspector Rice. Please have a seat. We appreciate your patience in waiting and we apologize for needing to speak to you again. We just have a few follow-up questions. What do you know of the Chinese girl? I'm told you spoke to her at the opening banquet."

"Briefly," I responded. "I found her to be a polite, hard-working girl."

"You were the only judge not affected by the alleged poisoning," he said.

"It was my good fortune that MacTavish's automaton broke down, which forced Lily to serve me. She was the one who noticed there was a problem."

"And how would she know that? She says she is twelve years old. How would a child know of such things?"

"Lily told me she noticed that MacTavish's entry had an unusual smell, and I believe her."

"I see. But why not say something earlier, if she was so concerned?"

"As I said, she didn't come close to the food until that moment."

"Did you notice anything unusual about the way the food looked or smelled?"

"No, I did not. But Lily did. She is personally acquainted with certain Oriental herbs that I have only read about."

"I see. Is there anything else you would like to add?"

"I'm sorry, that's all I know. May I ask you a question?"

The policeman regarded me curiously for a moment. "Certainly, what is it?"

"The chefs' assistants – what do you know of their backgrounds?"

"Why do you ask?"

"I'm just curious what credentials would be required to participate as an assistant."

The inspector eyed me skeptically. "What is this about?"

"My friend Emma observed him in the kitchens, acting in a hostile and secretive manner."

The inspector chuckled. "That would describe at least half of the chefs around here. Egomania is a job requirement, it seems. You are free to go, professor."

"Thank you, sir. And the girl, Lily. Is she free to go as well?"

"I don't know." He gestured to the other side of the stage. "The superintendent is speaking to her now."

I turned around and saw Lily, looking small and scared, speaking to St. James and another man at the other end of the stage.

"I will take responsibility for the girl," I said. "I'm concerned about her."

"Don't worry yourself about the likes of her, professor. I'm surprised the Exhibition staff even hired such a ragamuffin."

"Even so, please let me know when they've finished speaking with her."

"That wasn't much of an interrogation," Emma said when I returned and sat down beside her. "Do they suspect *you*?"

"Emma, *really.*"

"I'm just saying it might seem suspicious since you were the only judge who wasn't poisoned. They might think that you and the girl were in league."

As I tried to think of a reply, another policemen rushed in and interrupted the Superintendent's conversation with Lily. He lowered his voice and said something that made my heart sink.

"Ione, did you hear that?" Emma exclaimed. "Dame Leonora has passed away!"

"Goodness, that's horrible!" I exclaimed. "This is now a murder investigation."

"Now what?" Emma leaned back and placed her palm on her forehead as if she was nursing a headache. "This is a tragedy! It makes me very sad. Dame Leonora was a dear friend." She sniffled as a tear ran down her cheek. "Drat! I gave my hanky to Lily!"

I reached into my purse, grabbed my handkerchief, and handed it to her. "The perpetrator must be brought to justice."

"Hmm," Emma remained composed through her tears. "They're interviewing Fenimore's Chinese assistant right now. He looks shifty to me. Now he's one that I would suspect."

"Well, MacTavish and Fenimore are bitter rivals, and each of them accused the other. There is definitely bad blood between them."

"If Fenimore wanted to ruin MacTavish, he could have his assistant slip the herb into MacTavish's dish, and people would assume it was food poisoning. No one would ever set foot in his restaurant again."

But," I replied, "Since this was the final round, the King also got a taste of each dish. Poisoning the judges is one thing, but poisoning the king would prompt a thorough investigation. That would be high treason, wouldn't it?"

"Hmm," Emma replied. "But the King has a taster. Even if the metal man hadn't malfunctioned, the dish would never have gotten to him."

"True, assuming the taster had knowledge of wolfsbane. Its smell was masked under the strong flavor of curry. Even if King Edward never took a bite, it could be construed as attempted regicide."

"Look!" Emma said, drawing my attention. "They're letting him go. Why are they doing that? I bet he'll hop on the next boat out of here."

"Let's speak to Tom about this, perhaps he's heard something."

We got up and walked down to stage area where the interrogations were taking place.

"Ladies," said the young officer who had escorted us to our seats earlier, "This area is closed to the public."

"I'm with the press," Emma said, holding up her questionable credentials.

At that moment Tom approached us. He obviously had heard poor Leonora had died. Beneath his somber expression, I could detect a flicker of boyish excitement in his eyes. "Hello ladies," he said. "Quite a ghastly night, eh?"

"Certainly," I replied. "We have a question. Do you happen to know what happened with Fenimore's assistant, Lang Min?"

"They questioned and released him," O'Malley said with a shrug. "What of it?"

"No, old chum." Harrison had appeared at Tom's side, his pipe clenched in his teeth but currently unlit. "They said he could go for the moment, but he wasn't allowed to leave the building."

"But – he didn't appear to have any sort of guard," said Emma.

"Not to worry, there will be guards at all the exits," said O'Malley.

"Finally, they've released Lily." I hurried to meet her half way. She was wiping her wet eyes with Emma's handkerchief. "Are you alright?"

At my question, what was left of her composure evaporated. "They accused me of poisoning the judges," she sobbed and wiped her nose on the handkerchief. "I would never do that!"

"Now, now, everything is alright," I said, motioning for her to sit. "They had to question you, of course, but it's over now."

"Am I in trouble?" she sniffed. "Why did they tell me I can't leave?"

"Speaking of that," Harrison said, looking around. "Where did the Chinaman – what was his name again? Where did he go?"

Lily looked up, her eyes wide open. "Mr. Fenimore's helper?" Her eyes went wide, and she muttered something in Chinese.

"They let him go?" To Harrison, I said, "You said he wasn't allowed to leave."

"No, no, no!" Lily jumped up and ran for the door.

"Does that child ever walk anywhere?" Emma asked.

"Lily, come back!" I called, but she'd already hurried down the stairway to the main hall.

We pursue the suspect in a taxicab to the London Aeorodrome.
Illustration by José Cardeñas

Chapter 14. A Chase in Cabs

"Emma!" I rushed out the door with my friend following behind me.

"Ione?" Tom shouted after me. "Where on earth are you going?"

"Don't worry, Tom!" I called back, though I knew he would.

When we reached the bottom of the stairs, I broke into a run. Fortunately, the hallways were now deserted, and the young girl in the black and white uniform was easy to spot. "There she is!"

"Ione, slow down, I can hardly... keep up!" panted Emma. "These confounded shoes!" she paused to pull off her high-heeled footwear and continued in her stocking feet.

Lily disappeared into a door marked STAFF ONLY. I knew that if she encountered the matron, there would be trouble, but the bigger danger would be Lang Min. If he was indeed the culprit in the poisoning, he was no doubt capable of harming Lily as well.

As we dashed between the sinks and food preparation tables, we got plenty of stares from the workers who had been detained in the kitchen, currently playing card games. No one spoke to us or objected to our presence.

As I had expected, there was a police officer guarding the back door. "Ladies? Guests are not allowed in the kitchen area!" He seemed more exhausted than angry.

"We're just looking for... the lavatory!" I cried. Lily threw open a wooden door where a padlock hung open on a hasp at the top and headed into the storage room. As I glanced behind us, I was relieved that the bobbie had made no move to pursue us.

"Wait, Lily, stop!" I called after her.

The young girl ran between shelves piled high with jars, cartons, and boxes of food. At the end of the row, she made a sharp right and went through yet another door. There was darkness beyond. This egress to the outside was unguarded.

We followed her out onto a broad wooden platform which appeared to be a loading dock. The whole area was surrounded by a tall fence, with a gate on one end. I expected Lily to scramble over it, which would be easy given her youth, and quite difficult for us in our evening dresses. Instead, she produced a key from her pocket, unlocked the gate, and proceeded through.

"She has a key!" Emma exclaimed. "Brilliant!" As she ran to catch up to me, she dropped her shoes. She glanced back at them but kept running.

"Lily, please!" I called out. We hurried out through the unlocked gate.

When we caught up with her she was talking to a guard, a weary-looking man in the tuxedo uniform. "There, there, child, slow down, I can't understand ye. What's that you're saying?"

"The Chinese man! He's getting away!"

"What? What in blazes are you talking about?"

"She's with us,' I explained, panting, as Emma and I approached. "Did you happen to see a Chinese man come out of that gate and perhaps catch a taxi?"

Coming this time from an adult, he heard the question. "Maybe. What business is it of yours?"

"Here's a guinea for you," said Emma, still short of breath from running. She reached into her purse and placing the coin in his open hand. "Will that jog your memory?"

"Emma!" I scolded.

"It's alright, Ione, I read it in a book."

"I say, madam, that is much too generous!" he said as he deposited the coin in his pocket. "And yes, I did observe a Chinaman getting into one of those cabs from the Metropolitan Taxi Company, the ones painted black."

"They're all painted black," Emma said.

The man frowned. "I believe I overheard him asking to go to the aerodrome."

"Thank you, sir!" I cried. "Thank you very much!" I took the girl by the hand and said, "Come along, Lily. We'll do our best to catch him!"

Emma was already on the curb, waving and calling, "Taxi!" Several passed us by. She placed two fingers in her mouth in an attempt to whistle, but no sound came out. "How on earth do my boys do that?"

"Let me do it!" Lily pulled the whistle out from her blouse and blew a shrill blast. A rattling, wheezing motorcar pulled over to the curb.

"Clever girl," said Emma.

A plump, mustachioed man in a dark green uniform leaned out from the driver's seat in the front. "Yes, mum, where to?" he asked, looking us over.

"To the aerodrome, at once!"

"Beg pardon, miss, but I don't know if there's any flights leaving at this late hour."

"We are in a hurry!" I snapped.

"Have it your way, mum," he said. He got out and came around to open the passenger door. "Hop in."

As we climbed in the back seat, Emma giggled. "You sounded just like your mother."

"Really? I'll take that as a compliment. Now, when I was last in London," I said to Emma, "The aerodrome had not yet been constructed. What direction is it from here?"

"It's in the West End, not far away. We may catch him if we hurry."

All the while Lily sat silently between us, staring from one to the other.

"Young lady," I scolded her. "How could you have possibly thought to go after this man by yourself?"

Lily looked down. "Sorry, Miss Professor, but he was getting away. He knows all about *fu zi*, I'm sure. He is a horrible man. When I slipped and spilled water at the banquet, he cursed me in Chinese and called me a demon child. And I heard him tell someone how he used to work for the Scotsman, and how much he hated that man."

"I was not aware of that," I said. "No wonder he was glaring at MacTavish."

"Fascinating!" said Emma. "Not only did he have opportunity, but motive as well."

"Mr. MacTavish is rude and silly," Lily remarked. "But he's kind as well. He made sugar candy for the servers to eat."

"Tell us more about the poison," I said.

191

"Fu zi is very powerful. A tiny bit can fix many problems. But in the hands of a bad person..." She paused, choking on her emotions. "Mrs. Leonora was so kind to me," she sobbed.

I held her close. "There, there, we won't let him get away."

"There, ahead of us," cried Emma. "Another cab!"

"I see it! Driver!" I poked my head through the opening to the uncovered bench in the front where the driver sat. "We must catch up to that taxi!"

"Yes, mum," he said.

"I certainly hope that's the right one," said Emma. "I wish they didn't all look alike."

The black car ahead of us pulled up to the entrance to the aerodrome, a long curved path where several bobbies were pacing back and forth. We could see the bustle of the crowds under the stark electric light. Above was the silhouette of a great Zeppelin illuminated by floodlights. "It appears that they have night flights after all."

The black taxi pulled to the side and stopped.

"Driver!" I commanded. "Stop right here."

He did so and turned back to us. "Is this the place, ladies?"

"Just one moment," I said. "We have to be certain this is the man we're looking for."

Lang Min would not be difficult to spot; he would not have had time to change his exotic attire. No sooner had he emerged from the taxi when a pair of bobbies emerged from the gates. Our quarry turned and re-entered the vehicle, whereupon it made a wide circle in the entryway, almost colliding with another vehicle, which honked furiously. Before any of us could react, it zipped past us in the other direction.

"Oh, balls!" Emma exclaimed. "He's getting away!" Both Lily and I stared at her.

The man with the mustache turned back again to look at us. "Where to now, miss?"

"Turn around and follow that cab!"

"Yes, ma'am. Long as you've got money for the fare, I'll take you to Scotland if need be."

"That won't be necessary," Emma snapped. "But driving faster will!"

"I'll do my best, my good lady."

We rode on, the car's springs creaking and bouncing over the cobblestones.

To Lily I said, "What does the *fu zi* herb smell like?"

"It is the smell of freshly dug dirt," she said. "But also bitter. It is not easy to recognize unless you are a healer."

"Certainly MacTavish didn't know it," Emma chimed in. "I saw him lean over the stewpot and inhale the fragrance."

"Assuming the toxin was in the food and not just on the chopsticks," I said. "It would have had to been introduced in some other fashion, perhaps the serving bowls. What cook does not sample his cooking?"

"When you have been trained by a traditional healer," Lily said, "You learn to know the herbs. It is just like different diseases, which also have their own smell."

"Really?" I said. "That's fascinating."

"What if Lang Min were not the culprit?" Emma said, "Shouldn't he have recognized it? When MacTavish's entry was served, he had the most malevolent expression on his face. I assumed it was his hatred for the man, but maybe he found the smell distasteful."

"I saw that, too, but I'm quite sure he was staring at Angus. As Lily said, it replaced him."

"But it was MacTavish who built it," Emma argued. "As for Lang Min, if he is the poisoner, I don't see how he expected to get away with it. The new science of toxicology has made great strides in recent years. Surely an autopsy would show the cause of death."

"Why Emma, I had no idea you knew so much about such matters," I said.

"One can learn a lot from reading murder mysteries. Villains are very clever, but they always make a mistake that leads to their apprehension."

"These medicines are not well known in England," Lily said. "How do they tell what the poison was? Do they cut open the dead person's stomach?"

"Lily, that is not the sort of thing a young lady says," Emma scolded. "And yes, they can check the contents of the stomach, and also the blood. Most poisonings are substances like arsenic or strychnine that are easy to detect. Herbs might be more difficult."

"An experienced medical examiner should know the plant," I said. "Monkshood is commonly grown as an ornamental plant."

"That's true," Emma nodded. "Though I don't know why anyone would wish to grow something that was so poisonous."

"I suppose it would have had to be a subtle dose, to escape detection," I agreed. "If Lang Min is the guilty party, we certainly cannot let him get away."

"Ladies, how long should I continue following them? We're getting into an area that's quite dangerous for unaccompanied young women such as yourselves."

"Just keep driving," I said. "But stay back, we don't want to spook them."

The driver glanced back at me. "I think we already did that."

The cab we were pursuing rounded a corner and into an area where the gas streetlights were not illuminated.

"This does not look safe," said Emma.

"Should we still be following 'em?" our driver asked.

"Yes," I said. "We've come too far to let him get away now." We rounded that same corner the cab had just taken in time to see it turn yet again.

We followed our quarry along a street with a slight downward incline; our driver slowed and applied the brakes, which squealed as we descended. Gulls appeared overhead, telling me that we were nearing the river. I had assumed they were heading to the docks, but this was not the way. Just ahead of us, the road ended in a street that ran both ways to the left and the right. Along the street was a row of seedy-looking tenement houses.

"The Thames is just beyond those row houses," Emma explained.

"Judging by the smell," I said, "It must be quite ghastly to live there."

The Chinaman's cab stopped in front of one of the tenements. We watched him disembark and hurry down the walk, as the cab turned around and chugged away.

"Stop here," I told the driver.

"Alright then, your fare will be four shillings."

"Here's your four shillings," said Emma, handing him the coins, "and another four, if you agree to wait here until we return. I expect it shan't be long." She held out the extra coins near his hand.

"Well, I don't know," he said, taking the coins and glancing around. "Can't I dissuade you from this foolishness? I don't wish you ladies to come to harm."

"You're not afraid, are you?" said Emma. "If you don't wait as you agreed to do, I shall report you to your supervisor."

"I'm no coward," The man snapped, "But that don't mean I go in for no foolishness. I'll wait 30 minutes," he said, glancing at his pocket watch. "If you take longer than that, or if there's any trouble, I'll be gone before you can say lickety-split."

"We'll be quick," I muttered as we exited the taxi. "Now," I warned my companions as we hurried down the street, "Keep quiet and don't let them see you."

Fortunately, there was an automobile parked on the street a short way down the incline. "Emma, Lily," I pointed to the car, and we all crouched down behind it.

Lang Min stood at the dilapidated house, rapping on the door insistently. Every so often he paused and glanced around.

After two or three minutes of this, the door opened and another man stepped out. Though it was difficult to see him in the dim light, we were close enough to hear Lang address him in Chinese, whereupon he replied in the same language. The man turned to go back into the dwelling, but Lang grabbed the door and held it open before the man could shut him out.

"We need to get closer," whispered Emma. "I can't hear them!" Slowly she stood up from her crouching position.

"Stay down!" I warned her. "Look! Another car! Those men getting out are certainly not the Queen's cousins."

"I think, Ione, we are in trouble."

Professor Ione D. & the Epicurean Incident

The ruffians apprehend the unfortunate Lang Min as he
attempts to escape.
Illustration by José Cardeñas

Chapter 15. Dangerous Doings

Both my companions tried to get around me for a better view. "Where?" asked Emma.

"There!" cried Lily, then quickly lowered her voice. "That man, I've seen him before!"

I put a finger to my lips and whispered, "Let's just watch and listen."

On the street near the tenement sat a sleek black automobile. Though its engine was not running, the pings of its boiler cooling told me it had just arrived.

Whoever was inside the door shouted something in Chinese and punched at Lang, causing him to tumble down the stairs. The door to the tenement slammed shut, leaving Lang to the mercy of his pursuers. He scrambled to his feet and pounded on the door frantically. There was no response. In desperation, he began to shimmy up the drainpipe.

It was too late. The biggest of the three newcomers, a hulking gorilla of a man, bounded across the trash-strewn yard. He grabbed Lang by the collar and pried him off the pipe, detaching it from the building and sending it clattering to the ground.

"Gotcha, you slippery yellow devil! Thought you'd get away, didn't you?"

The tallest of the men wore a black derby with unkempt gray hair spilling out from under the brim. He gazed impassively at the struggling Asian. "It's pointless to resist, you know."

"Let me go!" Lang cried. "What you want from me?"

"If you don't know," laughed the third man, "You are one stupid bastard!"

Emma gasped and put her hands over Lily's ears, but the girl wriggled out of her grasp.

"Did you not think we were watching you?" Lang's captor growled. "Why in hellfire didn't you stay at the exhibition?"

"Emma, it's that horrible man!" I said, my voice an urgent whisper.

"What man?"

"The rude vendor with the potato machine."

"Good gracious, it is him! I knew he was no good the moment I laid eyes on him!"

"That's right, Chinaman," said another man's voice. "The coppers had nothing on you until you went and ran like a scared rabbit."

"Silence, Edgar," snapped the potato-chopper man in a calm yet menacing tone. "Do you want everyone on the river to hear you?"

Lang muttered something in Chinese.

"Yes, Mr. Lang," the man chuckled, "You are quite correct about Edgar's parentage."

"I can't believe he was so brazen to openly attend the Exhibition," Emma whispered.

"Hush!" I wondered what the man's motivation was. We had thought him a simple inventor, but clearly he had something much more sinister in mind than selling his creation.

"There was mistake," cried Lang Min. "Did not want to kill. I told you I know nothing of herbs. I did not mean for English lady to die!"

The two henchmen broke into cruel laughter.

Their leader held up a hand and they fell silent. "It was unavoidable in our situation," he said. "One cannot make a soufflé without first breaking eggs."

"Hungarian," I whispered to Emma. "That's what he sounds like."

"His cohorts are definitely English," she replied. "From the lower classes. What could be their connection?"

"So the rich bitch died, who gives a fig?" said the one called Edgar. "It's class warfare, us against them."

"That's right, Chink," said the third man. "Whose side you on, anyhow?"

"When will you learn to hold your tongues?" snapped the leader, cuffing each of them on the ear like a teacher disciplining impertinent schoolboys. "As for you," he addressed Lang, "You got your revenge. MacTavish is ruined."

"But... I did not want judges to die, just be sick! I thought you wanted to make fool of the King, to show English people he does not deserve to be ruler."

"Whatever gave you that idea? Surely you have as much reason as anyone to hate the monarchy, seeing how the imperialists corrupted your people with the poison of the poppy. Your so-called Boxers were correct. They did not just defend themselves, they cut the devils' throats."

There was a brief scuffle as Lang tried to break free from his captors, then cried out in pain as the two hoodlums tightened their grip on his forearms. "What you want from me?"

"You have become a liability to the cause. Edgar, Bill, hold him tightly, I shall return in a moment."

"No! Is not fair! I did what you wanted!"

The Hungarian turned back to his henchmen. "I'm finding this tiresome. Shut him up."

"No! Have mercy!" One of the men bound a dirty rag around Lang's mouth.

The Hungarian walked briskly to the car, opened up its boot and rummaged around, looking for something. He returned to his comrades with a coil of stout rope.

"Ione!" Emma said in an urgent whisper. "We can't sit by and let this happen."

"Agreed," I said. "Lang must have a fair trial."

"More importantly, I want to see them all brought to justice."

"One justice can overpower a hundred evils," whispered Lily.

"So it's hanging, then?" asked one of the henchmen, lowering his voice. "We could string 'im up on the lamp post, but it feels like half the world's watching."

"An astute observation, imbecile," the Hungarian mocked. "No, we shall bind his arms and legs and toss him in the Thames. We'll need something to weigh him down, but I'm certain we can find a big rock along the bank."

"Serves him right, since he bollixed the job," said one of the men, "The tyrant is still alive!"

"They were trying to kill His Majesty," Emma whispered. "It's as good as a confession!"

Lang managed to shrug off his gag. "No, no!" He began shrieking in Chinese until one of the henchmen fastened the rag again. With the two thugs holding him tightly, the Hungarian began binding Lang's arms with the rope.

"We must do something!" From her purse, Emma pulled out a tiny pearl-handled pistol.

"Emma, no!" I grabbed at her sleeve, but she had already jumped into the lamplight brandishing her weapon.

"Stop right where you are!" Emma shouted. "You are all under citizen detainment!"

"Mrs. Emma!" Lily cried.

"Hush!" I whispered, holding a finger to my lips.

Lily stared at me, open-mouthed. My friend's impulsiveness had put us all in extreme danger. I took a deep breath and collected my thoughts. Heart pounding, I withdrew my throwing knife from my boot.

"What a pleasant surprise!" sneered the Hungarian as he looked Emma's way, an evil grin on his face. "So you fancy yourself a detective? Edgar, disarm her!"

"Boss, she's got a gun!"

The leader laughed. "You call that thing a gun? It would scarcely kill a pigeon. Go!" He took hold of the partially bound Lang and shoved his underling in her direction.

The hoodlum hesitated only a second before charging at Emma. There was a loud crack as she pulled the trigger. The attacker gave a grunt of pain but didn't slow down in the slightest. He grabbed Emma's right arm, twisting her wrist until the gun fell with a clatter to the street. Her hat flew off as he wrapped his beefy arm around her neck and clapped a hand over her mouth. For a moment, he stood there panting, blood dripping from the wound in his shoulder.

"Damn you, woman!" Edgar gave a cruel laugh through clenched teeth, then hissed in pain. "What you say, boss, can I have a bit of fun with this one?"

"Is that all you think about?" the Hungarian retorted. "This is why I am in charge. Simply snap her neck and be done with it. You can have any trollop you want after this is over."

"I ain't never had a fine boozh-wah lady like this one," Edgar said, sniffing her hair. Emma shuddered and made a soft noise of disgust.

"Lily," I whispered, "Run, get the cabbie!" While the thugs continued their argument, I shucked off my boots so I could run quietly. Weapon in hand, I dashed down the shadowed side of the street.

At the same time, Emma bit her captor's forearm, kicked him in the shin, and stomped on his foot. He shouted a curse and released her, and she ran off down the street. "Bleeding twat bit me!"

"Get her," The Hungarian ordered. "I'll take care of the Chinaman!" He grabbed Lang Min and pinned him against a wall while Bill ran after Emma. "You, too, Edgar!"

While the ruffians were thus engaged I pocketed my knife then leapt from the shadows and dove for Emma's pistol. "Call off your dogs or I'll shoot!" I cried, holding the gun in the stance my father had taught me. "And I won't miss!"

"Go right ahead, pull the trigger," the Hungarian laughed. "That toy you're holding only holds a single bullet."

"Are you sure?" I said in an effort to bluff him. While I pondered my next move, Lang Min twisted free from the Hungarian's grasp and ran off in the other direction.

"Why you little yellow bastard," roared the wild-haired gang leader. He pulled something from his jacket and hurled it toward his quarry. Lang gave a shriek so loud that it was audible through his gag.

In the next instant, I felt a large body hit me and knock me to the ground. My head slammed onto the hard-packed street, causing an explosion of color behind my eyes. The gun fell to the ground once more, but I grabbed the knife from my vest pocket and stabbed the ruffian in the stomach. I pulled it out quickly, meaning to stab him again, but I was blocked as he gave a cry of pain and collapsed on top of me with his full weight.

The thug was far from immobilized. He grabbed at my knife with one hand and struck me in the chin with the other. Rather than surrender my weapon, I tossed it to the side, and attempted to strike his nether regions with my knee. Though I barely connected, he quickly jumped off and out of the way. Despite his tough demeanor, he was truly a coward. I scrambled back and retrieved the knife.

"You're a feisty one," he grunted, assuming a wrestler's stance as I held him at bay with the bloody blade.

I struggled to my feet, slashing at Bill, causing him to back off as he clutched at his bleeding stomach. My father's voice rang in my mind. "The first rule of self-defense is to run for your life," he'd said, but I couldn't do that until Emma was out of danger. Where was she?

I found out momentarily. "Release me at once!" she shouted as Edgar dragged her back toward the tenement. His shirt was soaked with blood on the shoulder where Emma had shot him, but he didn't seem to notice. I thought I might knock down her captor if I could charge him before he could react, but he stopped me in my tracks.

"Take one more step, missy," Edgar hissed, holding a jagged blade beneath Emma's chin, and your friend loses her head, understand?" With his other hand, he pressed Emma against a wall. I could see her face in the moonlight, white with terror.

I looked around and considered my options. The Hungarian was gone, pursuing Lang Min. My attacker was wounded, but not incapacitated. I heard him grunt in pain as he staggered in my direction. I whirled around to face him.

"Give us the knife, tart," rasped Bill from behind me, "And after we've had a bit of fun with you two, we'll let you go."

"Stay back!" I shouted, waving the blade at him. "Or you will regret it!"

He laughed, then groaned. "Edgar," he called to his compatriot, "If she sticks me again, you cut the other one's throat."

"If you harm her in any way, I shall kill you!" I cried, surprising myself with how calm my voice sounded. "I'm not afraid of you, and I'm not leaving without her."

"My husband is a member of Parliament," Emma cried. "If you let us go unharmed, you may avoid the gallows."

"For God's sake, just cut her throat, Edgar!" boomed a voice from down the street. It was the Hungarian, dragging Lang Min. Despite being half out of his bonds, the Chinaman was limp and unresisting.

Before I could react to the new threat, a sudden noise made me look up. A motorcar chugged down the street in our direction, its one intact headlight shining in our eyes. From within the vehicle came a long, loud whistle.

"This is the police!" shouted an odd-sounding voice. "Drop your weapons!"

"Hellfire and damnation!" snapped Edgar.

The car's tires crunched on the gravel as it picked up speed. While the thug was distracted, Emma swooned and slipped through his arms to the ground. I scrambled to get out of the way, barely escaping being run down as I stumbled on the loose rock. As the vehicle hurtled past me, a small form flew at me, knocking me to the ground and ripping the hem of my dress.

Before I could discern who and what had hit me, and what had happened to Emma, there was the sound of a crash and an agonizing shout.

"Lily!" I struggled to a sitting position, hugged her for a second, then remembered my friend. "Emma! Emma!" I shouted.

"Ione!" cried Emma, now running toward us. "Lily! How? What?"

I jumped up to see what had happened. The car, the same one we had hidden behind, had bounced up the front steps and slammed into the brick wall of the tenement building. The wall was cracked but intact. The upper half of the hoodlum's body lay, unmoving, on the car's bonnet.

As I snatched Emma's gun from the ground, she cried. "Ione, behind you!"

I felt two rough hands grab me, one on my waist and the other on my wrist, in an attempt to wrest the gun from my grip. Despite the loss of blood, Bill was still very strong and I knew I would not be able to surprise him a second time.

"No!" screamed Lily. The girl was a blur of motion as she leapt up to strike my attacker with something. I heard glass breaking and a wet-sounding thud. The man grunted in surprise and released his grasp, allowing me to escape. He stood dazed and swaying, blood gushing from the gash in his head. Lily stood beside me, brandishing the jagged remains of a discarded wine bottle.

"Don't you dare take one step closer," I warned him, waving my knife. I tossed the gun to Emma, and she caught it.

"God damn it all!" cried the Hungarian, throwing Lang to the ground. "How did these... *women* get the best of you fools?"

Lang lay on the ground motionless, a knife protruding from his back.

"Let's cut their throats!" Edgar cried. "Throw 'em in the river!"

"This is finished! You are through!" I shouted. "The police are on their way!"

Edgar advanced slowly, then stopped, as if unsure of himself. I was brandishing my knife and Emma her gun. Even Lily was armed with the broken bottle. I'm sure we were a curious trio.

The sound of a siren interrupted the unbearable tension. Two motorcars with police markings roared down the street and stopped just in front of us with a spray of gravel. "That's him! He's the one!" I cried, pointing at the Hungarian who was just disappearing into the darkness between the tenements.

My heart jumped in my chest when Lang Min suddenly moved. He struggled to his knees and managed to free his arms, then raised them in the air when he realized the police were aiming their guns at him. I was dumbfounded to see that the Hungarian's knife was still embedded in his backside.

"Stop in the name of the law!" A policeman cried as he ran after the Hungarian, blowing his whistle repeatedly.

Another bobbie rushed over to apprehend the big man whom I had stabbed. The criminal had been unable to run without staggering. "Now be a good lad and let me get these cuffs on you," he said. "My, my, who did this? Looks like you got mauled by a bear." When the policeman looked our way, his mouth fell open in astonishment, which turned into a grin.

"Good evening, constable," I said as I tucked the knife back in my vest pocket. "As you can see, we've had a bit of trouble."

Lily dropped the broken bottle and embraced me. Emma quickly hid the gun in her purse and picked up her hat from where it had fallen to the street. "Oh dear," she said as she examined it. "I think I've lost a songbird."

A third man emerged from the police car, not in uniform but in the white pants and jacket of a chef. "Miss Dfrdwy! Mrs. Farrington!"

"Neville Montague?" I cried in surprise.

"Mr. Montague," Emma echoed. "What in blue blazes are you doing here?"

Neville looked me up and down. "Good Lord, Professor you're bleeding! We must call for a doctor at once!"

"We're fine!" I said, exhaling in exasperation. "It's nothing a bit of iodine and a bandage or two won't cure."

"You're lucky the two of you weren't killed, after acting so recklessly!"

"Your assistance is most appreciated," Emma said. "But... how?"

"When I realized you'd gone," Neville explained, "I went to the police immediately and was able to convince them to follow your taxicab. Unfortunately, we lost you in your sudden roundabout at the aerodrome."

"I still don't understand," Emma said. "A chef leading a rescue?

"That's because you're not really who you say you are," I said. "Am I right?"

Lily nodded in agreement.

"So you're not a chef?" Emma exclaimed.

"Neville Montague," I said, "Are you or are you not a clandestine operative of the Metropolitan Police?"

Emma's mouth fell open in surprise.

Montague laughed. "I suppose it's useless to keep up the charade anymore. There were rumors that there might be a threat on His Majesty's life, so I was assigned to participate in the contest and keep an eye on things."

"Yet you managed to get all the way into the finals. If I had not been a judge, I might suspect that the contest was rigged."

"What I said about my family's restaurant and reputation is true. I have indeed had much experience in the kitchen, though if not for the help of my sister..."

"Who's this, then?" cried the constable, pointing down the street.

A cab had pulled up next to the police cars. One of the doors opened, and Thomas and Harrington emerged.

We must appear to be a curious trio.
Illustration by José Cardeñas

Chapter 16. A Culprit Captured

"Ione!" Tom rushed over and gave me a crushing embrace. "Thank heavens you're safe! What were you thinking, pursuing those dangerous criminals? Where are your boots? And... Blessed Mother Mary, you're bleeding!"

"Tom," I replied, stepping back for air, "I'm fine, we're fine. We have the situation well in hand," My hand went up to my hair; in all the excitement I hadn't realized there was blood dripping down from my scalp. "It's only a flesh wound, nothing more."

He looked over at Emma. "You, too? Why is everyone bleeding?"

Emma straightened herself up and said, in as dignified a manner as possible, "The perpetrator fled the scene of the crime. We couldn't allow him to escape justice."

"But these are dangerous criminals!" Tom cried. "You could have been killed."

"We had no idea that Lang Min, Fenimore's assistant, was in league with these ruffians. It appeared at the time to be simple revenge, professional jealousy. As for the location of my boots... I'm afraid I don't know."

"I don't think I will ever fully understand..." Tom's fair face was flushed in anger, which turned to amusement as he saw Emma's stocking feet. He shook his head. "What the two of you did was terribly reckless. The police were seeking the Chinese lass. Is she with you?"

"Here are your boots, Miss Professor." Lily emerged from the shadows, footwear in hand.

"I was indeed foolhardy," Emma said. "I got caught up in the heat of the moment. But what a story! My sons will not believe the adventure their mother has had!"

"That's all well and good," Harrison chimed in. "But you're quite lucky the police arrived when they did. And who's this? One of the contest finalists?" He pulled a notepad from his jacket and headed for Neville, subjecting him to a barrage of questions.

I replied to Tom's incredulous look. "Mr. Montague is a police operative."

"Such a dashing young man," Emma said. "I should have known he was more than a mere cook."

Tom was about to say something when the Superintendent approached us. "I would be remiss if I did not admonish you ladies for your recklessness. Nevertheless, we owe a debt of gratitude to you, Professor D. and Mrs. Farrington, for your bravery in apprehending the perpetrators.

And... Great Scott, you're bleeding! Constable, the ladies require first aid."

"It's not necessary," I said. "And we are very happy to have helped bring Dame Leonora's killer to justice. Though it appears she was not the intended target."

"It was a conspiracy!" Emma interjected. "An evil conspiracy of assassination!"

"In any case," St. James continued, "I'm relieved that no one else was harmed." He turned to see one of the bobbies returning alone from down the street, breathing quite heavily. "O'Reilly, report. Where is Johnson?"

"We lost the suspect, sir. Johnson is still searching."

"Professor, what do you know about the third man?" St. James asked me.

"He was a vendor at the Exhibition," I replied. "Emma and I encountered him while browsing through the kitchen devices. His attitude was unusual, to say the least."

"Unusual, you say?"

"Superintendent, may I have a word?" called one of the bobbies. He had been examining the unfortunate Bill. "You need to see this."

St. James glanced back and sighed. "Just a moment, ladies." While he went over to check on the injured criminal, I pulled on my boots.

Despite my earlier relief, it now felt as if there was a rock in my stomach. Emma's face went white, and Lily embraced me, her eyes brimming with tears.

"What on earth is the matter?" Tom asked.

"It will be alright, Lily," I said.

In a moment, St. James confirmed our fears. "The suspect has died."

"What happened to him?" Tom asked.

"He was crushed between the car and the wall. Professor, this wasn't an accident, was it?"

"Yes, it was, in the sense that his death was unintentional. But that horrible man was holding a knife to Emma's throat. I was helpless to save her. Young Lily started the motorcar and used it as a distraction to allow Emma to get away."

"What this brave young lady did saved my life," Emma said. "That ruffian would have killed me, or worse. I was sure it was my last night on earth, and I was saying my final prayers when those headlamps suddenly appeared. I will gladly testify on Lily's behalf."

"I'm sure she meant to deter the man rather than harming him. Isn't that right, Lily" I stroked the girl's hair as she hid her face in my dress.

The superintendent's stern face softened. "There, there, young miss, I can't believe any magistrate who's got a lick of humanity would bring charges against a brave young lass such as yourself. Considering these ladies' testimony I believe this to be an accident." He bent down to pat Lily on the head.

"Captain, what do we do with 'im?" said one of the officers, dragging a sullen, handcuffed Chinaman in our direction. "I must see barrister," snapped Lang Min as they brought him to where we were standing. "You arrest me because I am Chinese." He followed that with a series of vile-sounding exclamations in his language, which made Lily's eyes go wide.

"That's got nothing to do with it," said the superintendent. "You fled in defiance of police orders. You are at the least a witness to a murder."

"I poison no one!" Lang continued ranting and raving in his own language as the constable forced him into the back of the police wagon.

Lily looked at me. "He is lying. And he just called them all sorts of bad names."

"We spoke to Chef MacTavish," said Harrison. "He was adamant that Mr. Lang was not the sort to commit murder. I believe his words were, 'Bloody coward wouldn't have it in him.'"

"MacTavish?" Lang's face, visible through the barred window of the back seat of the police car, reddened in fury. "He stole my recipes, and gave no credit! He promised I be rich and famous! Became wealthy off my work!"

"There's your motivation," said Tom. "Professional jealousy."

The Chinaman ceased his ranting. His face disappeared from the window.

"He certainly appears to be the culprit," Harrison said. "Even if he didn't intend to kill anyone. But what is his connection to this troop of blackguards?"

"King Edward was indeed their target," I explained, "Even if Mr. Lang was not aware of it. It was quite ingenious how he coated the chopsticks with poison, which is something the royal taster would have missed. The ringleader, whom I believe is Hungarian, was going on about shedding blood for some revolutionary cause."

"One of the others said, 'The tyrant is still alive,'" Emma added.

"If it was attempted regicide," Harrison said, "Surely these conspirators will hang."

"Ione, I've arranged for the taxi driver who brought us here to take you ladies back to the hotel," O'Malley said. "Please stay in your room and lock your door, since this Hungarian fellow is still at large."

"Thank you, Tom," I said. Normally his solicitude would have offended me, but I was far too tired to argue.

Emma, Lily, and I rode back to our hotel, utterly exhausted. Lily quickly fell asleep in my lap. "I swear that I will find a good home for you," I whispered, "and for all your friends that have been sleeping on the streets."

"Nigel and I would be happy to adopt her," Emma said quietly. "I would be proud to have such a clever, brave girl as a daughter."

"As would I," I said.

The next morning, Emma, Lily, Tom, and I sat down to breakfast in the hotel's dining room. "Mrs. Emma, you have decorated your bandages," Lily smiled. "They are quite lovely."

"Thank you." Emma had tied colorful ribbons on the bandages on her arm and neck. She had used an additional ribbon to conceal where the songbird was missing from her hat.

"I'm envious," I said, pushing up my hair. "All I have are these scalp wounds with these unsightly iodine stains."

Tom shook his head, then quickly changed the subject. "I'm famished," he declared. "After all the incredible food at the Exhibition, I thought I wouldn't need to eat for a week."

"They're serving eggs Benedict and toast, one of my favorites," I said. "Did you and Harrison discover any new information after we departed?" I asked Tom.

"Doctor Lacrosse confirmed there was wolfsbane in the curry, and on the chopsticks" he replied. "Which supports Miss Lily's story."

"And there were dual motives," I added. "Given that Mr. Lang felt MacTavish treated him unfairly, and the Hungarian's group wanted to assassinate King Edward."

"I wonder how Mad MacTavish will feel about being called to testify," said Emma.

Tom smiled, "I can imagine he'll say, "This is most unfair. I've got a restaurant to run!'"

We laughed. "You do a very impressive Scottish accent," I said.

"The mechanical man," said Lily. "It cannot talk, can it?"

"Of course not," I said, smiling at her girlish innocence. "Which is why it can't complain about being underpaid."

Lily nodded. "Did the police find any of the medicines?" she asked Tom.

"They searched the Chinaman's bag, which they found near that tenement. Inside was a sack filled with vials of colored powders. He claimed they were spices, but of course, the police have taken them to their laboratory for further testing. Wolfsbane would not be so obvious as arsenic or cyanide, but knowing what to look for, the inspectors will find it."

"Mr. Lang can hardly plead ignorance of the attempted regicide," Emma said. "He knew how the contest was structured."

"I'm not so certain Lang Min knew about the King's participation," I countered. "I do believe he thought the victims would only be sickened, not killed."

Lily looked up at Tom, her mouth drawn and face pale. "I feel horrible about the man I hit with the motorcar."

"Put that nonsense out of your mind, young lady," said Tom. "He was a criminal who reaped the consequences of his actions. In any case, your quick thinking prevented him from taking Mrs. Farrington's life."

"You're a heroine, Lily," said Emma.

"Hear, hear!" I added.

"Then... may I please go?" She looked at us, pleading with her dark eyes.

"Where do you want to go?" I asked her.

Her gaze fell. "To see my friends, Susie and little Henry and the others. I've been quite worried about them."

"Others?" Tom asked. "Do you mean your friends in the orphanage?"

"There is no orphanage," I said. "Lily and her friends have been living on the streets."

"We stay in an abandoned shop," she said. "There are five of us; Susan and Henry, along with Edward and Sam."

Emma's mouth fell open. "You children have been living on your own? Where do you get food?"

"We get scraps behind hotels and pubs. Sometimes we beg for coppers to buy bread."

Tom shook his head. "What deplorable circumstances. Not even a place to bathe!"

"There's a fountain in the park," she said. "We run through it in our clothes until the old man comes to chase us away."

"How resourceful!" I said.

"One time, Mr. MacTavish saw me taking food home from the Exhibition. He was going to have me sacked until I told him about the others. He gave me ten loaves of bread but warned me to tell no one."

"He would hate to acquire a reputation for generosity," laughed Tom.

Emma said, "I simply won't hear of you and your friends living on your own even one night longer. I promise we will find you all proper homes."

"Perhaps Harrison can help," Tom said with a smile. "This is just the kind of story that would catch the attention of his readers."

"That would be wonderful," Emma said. "But even if he doesn't take up the cause, my Nigel and I know plenty of people who will."

"Then we are agreed," I said to my companions, "The first matter at hand is to see to it that Lily's friends are safe."

"Regrettably," Tom said, "I need to send my employers a telegram concerning last night's events. I expect to see Harrison shortly afterward, and I'll request his help in this matter."

"That will be wonderful, Tom. Emma, will you accompany us?"

"I would be delighted," she replied with a grin.

The three of us left the hotel and hailed a taxicab which took us to Charing Cross, to the abandoned shop where her friends were currently residing.

We entered the shop from the alley, through a back door with a broken latch. Only Edward, aged eight, was present. "We thought you were gone forever!" he cried as he hugged Lily. By nightfall, we had located the other three children, three boys and another girl, ranging in age from five to nine years.

The orphans regarded Emma and me with suspicion, but with Lily's help, we were able to gain their trust. She was the eldest of the group, all of whom addressed her as 'Miss Lily.'

It was not easy to find a cab large enough to accommodate all of us. Furthermore, Lily's friends were ragged and unkempt, with dirt-smudged faces. After being rejected by several taxis, we encountered one with a female driver, who took pity on the children and offered to take us to the Exhibition for free. Emma insisted on paying anyway, and I added a generous tip.

The Exhibition guards refused to allow us inside with our ragged charges. Emma was livid. "This is Professor Ione D., who helped to capture the scoundrels who tried to kill His Majesty. I insist you send for Mr. Wagstaffe at once."

When Wagstaffe arrived with Tom and Harrison in tow, he apologized profusely and admitted us to the Crystal Palace.

"Superintendent St. James spoke with the vicar of his parish," Harrison said. "He is sending a patrol car to take them to the church to be washed and fed."

"The reverend and his wife have promised to find homes for all of them," Tom added.

It was a tearful farewell when the police sergeant arrived to take Lily's friends to the church. They were frightened at first but Lily convinced them they were not going to jail.

That evening at the hotel, Lily awoke in the wee hours of the morning. She huddled at the end of her cot, shaking and crying.

"What's wrong, dear?"

"That horrible man," she sobbed. "The boss. In my dream, he came to our hiding place and threw Edward, Susie, Henry and Georgie in the river!"

"There, there," I said. "It was just a dream, and your friends are safe. You were very brave and we are all proud of you."

"Thank you, Miss Professor."

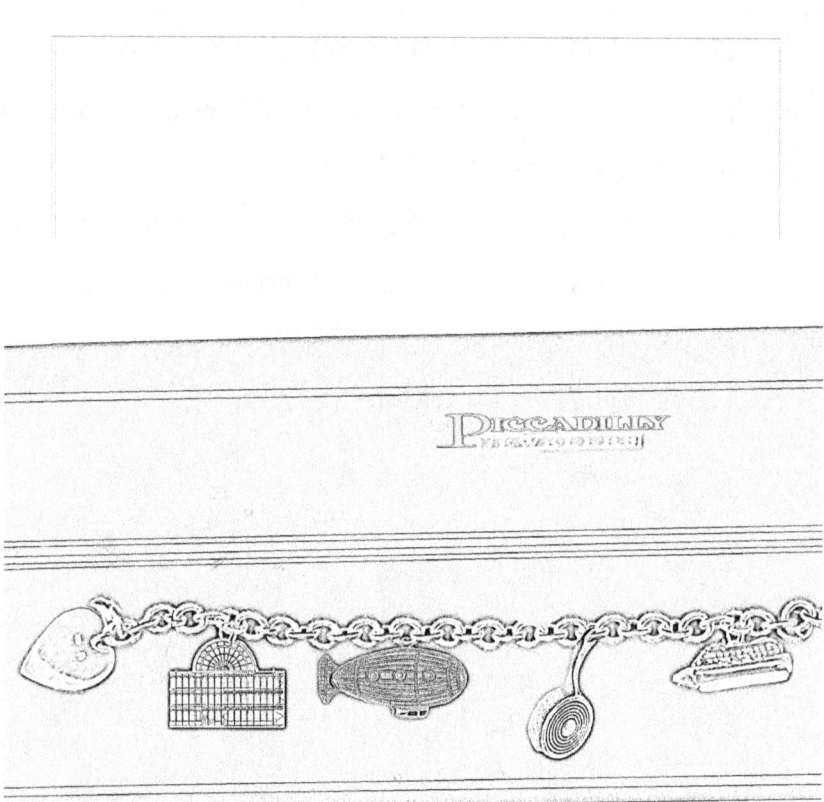

Emma presents Lily with a charm bracelet as a
memento of the Exhibition.
Illustration by Vaughn Treude

Chapter 17. Epicurean Epilogue

The following day, Tom, Emma, Lily and I took a horse-drawn carriage back to the police station for the Borough of Lambeth, not far from the Crystal Palace. We arrived to see a big commotion out in front, with at least a dozen reporters clamoring to be let in.

"I hope we can get through this crowd," I said.

A whiff of smoke caused me to look around. Harrison had just walked up from behind us, accompanied by a uniformed officer. "Oh, there you are. The police are anxious for another interview. I trust you've all rested from the other night's adventure?"

"Quite well, thank you," said Emma. "I could have probably slept through the day, had Ione not roused me for breakfast."

"Has there been any word about Sir Phillip?" I asked Harrison as the crowd parted

"He is still ill but recovering. It's a real tragedy that the doctors didn't know what was happening, or they might have been able to save Dame Leonora,"

"Where are the suspects?" asked Tom.

"They're being held at the Newgate," Harrison replied, "Miserable, decaying place that it is, it's quite appropriate for them." He took a puff from his pipe and said, "As for you, Professor, I expect you'll be called to testify in the trial; you, too, Mrs. Farrington."

"Yes, I suppose," I said. "I was so looking forward to getting back to my humdrum life as a professor."

I hoped they could take my testimony quickly, as I was quite anxious to return to the College. Before I could do that, there was yet another pressing matter to be resolved.

As we entered through the big wooden doors to the station, Tom said, "We were discussing the matter of Lily, and the other homeless orphans that we took to the vicar's. As we said last evening, because of all the scandals that have come out of the Exhibition, this would be an excellent way to end this event in a positive light."

Harrison grinned. "I'd be delighted to do whatever I can. I will ask around. I have connections, you see."

"As for you, Miss Lily, my boys have always wanted a little sister," Emma said. "Though perhaps they could have an older sister instead if you'd consent to come live with us."

Lily looked sad for a moment, then quickly recovered her composure and smiled. "I am most honored that you would be willing to have me. But I would feel terrible to impose on your household." She looked at me with sad brown eyes.

"I'm sure it would not be an imposition, Lily," I said. "Emma is my dearest friend and a wonderful lady, with a fine husband and two darling little boys. I'm sure you will love them."

"That's right," Emma said. "Another child would only add more happiness to our family."

"You are so kind and generous." Lily hugged Emma and me. I wiped a tear from my eye.

"There is so much for a young lady to do on our estate – hiking and horse-riding, fishing, archery, lawn tennis, and of course, the best education." Emma looked down at Lily, and at me, then shook her head. "On second thought, no. No, this simply will not do."

"What?" I asked, puzzled.

"I'm afraid I simply can't take her."

"Why not?" Lily asked, looking back and forth between us.

"I just realized," Emma explained, "That I was being very selfish, to contemplate separating the two of you. It is you, Ione, who need Lily to keep you out of trouble. Right, Lily?"

I gave them both a broad smile. "Well, I suppose, if you say so, Emma."

Lily grabbed me in a tight embrace and I wept in joy and relief. I looked up at Emma, and Tom who were wiping away tears. Even Harrison turned away to scrutinize a potted plant.

We had not waited long before Detective Neville Montague greeted us, wearing a handsome tweed suit. The anteroom was dominated by a huge desk with a uniformed bobbie sitting behind it. Police officers went hither and yon, some escorting handcuffed criminals.

"Greetings, everyone, Professor Dfrdwy," Montague said. "Follow me please, and we'll take you all to a more comfortable place where we will interview each of you."

"I shall be most delighted to do whatever I can to serve the cause of justice," Emma said. Lily was silent and wide-eyed as we followed Neville past the front desk into a long hallway.

I was not surprised that Neville Montague had arranged to be my interviewer. His tone throughout was businesslike. He avoided eye contact as we reviewed the questions we had gone over the night of the poisoning. A young male secretary sat by his side, recording my answers.

"And now," I said, "I would like to ask you a question. I was wondering if the man with the Hungarian accent has been apprehended."

Montague glanced at the secretary, who nodded and closed his notebook. "I can tell you, but this is off the record, as they say. We have not yet been cleared to speak of this to the press."

"Yes, I promise to keep it in confidence," I replied.

"We believe that the ringleader whom you encountered was Istvan Koezismert, a notorious Marxist revolutionary from Austria-Hungary. We are undertaking a nationwide search for the man."

"Goodness! Is that the man who escaped from the notorious prison in Spielberg Castle?"

"The very same. Though he hails from an aristocratic background, he has pursued a career of violence and terror across the Continent."

"That makes sense," I replied. "I have read of these Marxists, and they have a singular hatred for hereditary monarchs."

"Apprehending this man is our top priority, Professor."

Not until the very end did he repeat the question he had asked me twice over the last few days. "Professor D., would you accompany me to dinner?"

As he looked at me with his smoldering dark eyes, I could feel my cheeks flush.

"My goodness, Detective Montague, do you think that's a proper way to end an interview, by inviting the subject to dinner? Did you ask Mr. O'Malley the same question?"

"Sadly, he rejected me," Neville replied with a hearty laugh.

"What do *you* think?" I addressed the secretary.

The young man glanced at Neville and then back to me. "I really couldn't say, miss."

"Alright, then, Mr. Montague. I accept your invitation. Since I've taken charge of young Miss Lily, I hope it will be alright if she comes with us."

Without hesitation, he replied, "She will be most welcome."

With the Exhibition concluded and his reporting on the so-called "Lamb Curry Affair" completed, O'Malley was called back to New York. Sadly, I was not able to see him off, but he sent me a telegram explaining that he'd had urgent matters to attend to, and that he would see me back in the States.

❀❀❀❀❀

The following evening was our dinner with Montague, at the finest French restaurant in London. Neville was a perfect handsome gentleman and treated us both to a wonderful meal of boeuf bourguignon and truffle salad with a dessert of crepes Suzette. We shared some delightful conversation in which he was thoughtful enough to include Lily. I asked Neville of his upbringing in a restaurant family, and of how he became involved in law enforcement.

"I have always loved food and cooking," he said. "But since I was small I have also loved dime novels and the exciting way they portrayed law enforcement. I knew that being a policeman was the only occupation for me."

Afterwards, Neville gave the two of us a ride to our hotel in his steam car. He held the door for us as we disembarked, then gave me a kiss on the cheek and Lily a kiss on the forehead.

"Would you write to me after your return to America?" he asked.

"I will," I promised.

❀❀❀❀❀

The next morning, Emma and I said farewell at the train station.

"The Exhibition turned out to be far more hectic than we expected," I said.

"And great fun," she said. "But I'm quite anxious to return to my family. I'm sure the house is a shambles. I shall miss you, Ione."

"I miss you already," I said, a tear running down my cheek.

"And you, brave Lily," Emma said, embracing her. "You are a wonderful little lady and I'm sure that you will accomplish great things in your life."

"Thank you," the girl sniffed.

"I have something for you," Emma continued. She handed Lily a tiny velvet box, which she eagerly opened.

"A bracelet!" she cried. "I have never had one."

"It's a charm bracelet," Emma explained. "These little pendants are mementos of your time at the Exhibition. This one represents the Crystal Palace and this is a cooking pot. As you have more adventures you can add more charms to help you remember them."

"Oh Emma," I exclaimed. "What I wonderful idea! Just like the ones we have."

"How beautiful!" Lily explained. "I wish I had a gift for you."

"You do," Emma smiled, "Promise me one thing."

"What is it?"

"Take good care of Ione."

Lily nodded in utmost seriousness. "I agree to take on the challenge."

Emma laughed and gave her a hug. "There's a good girl."

"Just imagine what Nigel and the boys will say when you tell them of your adventures at the Exhibition," I said.

"For once, they will willingly listen to one of my stories," Emma said with a laugh. "Though I may leave out the details of my foolhardy behavior. And now I have something for you, Ione."

"For me?"

Emma opened her purse and retrieved a piece of paper, which she unfolded and handed to me.

"Why, Miss Professor, it's you!" Lily exclaimed.

"Where did you get this?" The sketch was a perfect likeness of me, seated at the judges' table on the evening of the final contest. "It's wonderful."

"The artist's signature is in the corner," Emma said with a smile.

The sketch was signed 'Tomas O' Malley' and entitled, 'Of Beauty and Love.'

❀❀❀❀❀

Then there was the matter of Lang Min's upcoming trial. Montague arranged for me to give my testimony in advance to the magistrate so I could return to my duties as a professor. When this matter was complete, I took this opportunity to inquire about obtaining custody of Lily.

Lily's status as a subject of the British Empire was unclear, with no proof of her paternity, though she had been told her father was an English sailor. As Lily had no known relations, the magistrate was quite willing to expedite the matter of guardianship for the heroine of the vile conspiracy against His Majesty.

All that remained now was to secure transportation for the journey back to America. My parents had sent funds to a local bank so I could purchase tickets for the trans-Atlantic Zeppelin. It was considerably more expensive than travel by ship would have been, but I was obliged to return to my classes before the semester commenced.

"I can't believe I am going to live in yet another country. From China where I was born, over the seas to England, and now I will travel to America. I am most grateful to you, Professor Diff-er-dwee."

Her words made me smile, not only for the sentiment but because for the first time, she had pronounced my surname correctly.

"I must thank you as well. You shall be my companion and assistant, which I appreciate greatly. But please," I scolded, "No more calling me 'Miss D' or 'Professor.' I would prefer that you address me as Ione."

"Yes, Miss Ione." Lily grinned. Together we left the courthouse and returned to the hotel, where we gathered our belongings and caught another taxi. On our ride to the Aerodrome, Lily kept a nervous silence until we were near enough to spot a great Zeppelin floating above us.

"There!" she cried. "Is that the one that will take us to America?"

"Yes," I said. "The view is unbelievable. And I've gotten one more thing to keep you busy on our journey." I unwrapped a large package and produced a sketch pad and several pencils. "I have had scant time for my artistic pursuits, but if you're interested, I would be happy to show you how to draw."

"I would like that, Miss Ione," she grinned.

I finally get to see what Tom was working on. The
sketch is entitled, 'Of Beauty and Love.'
Illustration by Suzanne Stewart

About The Authors

Vaughn Treude grew up on a farm in North Dakota and has been reading science fiction and fantasy as long as he can remember. In 2012, he published his first novel, Centrifugal Force, about computer hackers who overthrow the US government. Since then he has concentrated on steampunk, writing Fidelio's Automata and co-authoring the "Professor Ione D." series of young adult novels with his wife Arlys Holloway. Vaughn and Arlys are also co-creators of the musical comedy One Good Man, which is loosely based on Arlys' experiences in the on-line dating world. To learn more about Vaughn, check out his blog at steampunkdesperado.com.

Arlys Holloway was raised in Glendale, Arizona, when it still had a small-town western feel. She hails from a long line of women named Arlys, including her mother and daughter. She created the character Ione D. for Facebook posts promoting Vaughn Treude's novel Fidelio's Automata, but the character took on a life of her own. Arlys is the co-author of Miss Ione D and the Mayan Marvel and Professor Ione D and the Epicurean Incident. Arlys and Vaughn also created the play One Good Man, a comedy about on-line dating, which is appropriate since that is how they met.

Vaughn L. Treude & Arlys-Allegra Holloway

**Professor Ione D. and the Steam-Powered Minotaur,
Coming from Nakota Publishing in 2018
Illustration by Kyle Dunbar**

Preview: Professor Ione D. and the Steam-Powered Minotaur
by Vaughn Treude & Arlys-Allegra Holloway
Over the Aegean Sea, 1902
Chapter 1. Maelstrom

Lily stared at the blank page on her sketch pad and selected a pastel chalk from her case. "What shall I draw, Miss Ione?"

"Whatever comes into your mind," I said. "We've seen many wonderful things on our journey. How about the gorgeous view on this beautiful day?" The two of us sat in the observation lounge of the Zeppelin *Maria Theresa*. Below us stretched the dazzling blue of the Aegean Sea.

"It is beautiful," Lily admitted. "But there's nothing to draw, just the water."

"Those clouds to our port side are quite impressive," I said. "See how the sunlight brings out all the different shades of gray."

Lily turned in her chair to get a better look. It had been ten months that she had been my ward, in which time she had blossomed from a shy Anglo-Chinese orphan to a proper young lady. In the frilly ochre dress my mother had bought her, she radiated an exotic beauty. Unlike many girls her age, however, she preferred great literature and the natural sciences to fancy clothes, parties, and boys. "Those are cumulonimbus clouds," she said. "I hope it won't storm."

As if on cue, the captain's voice rang out, startling me somewhat as we were sitting directly beneath the speaker tube. "Ladies and gentleman, we are approaching an unexpected thunderstorm. For your safety, we will be taking a wide berth, but in case we encounter an atmospheric disturbance, please secure yourself and your belongings and extinguish all smoking materials."

"Look!" cried a lady sitting near us, pointing out the viewport. "Lightning! If it hits the airship, will we explode?"

"It's alright, ma'am," Lily said. "This airship is equipped with the new De Mores design. There's an outer bag with a layer of helium around the hydrogen. Helium isn't flammable at all."

"Still..." The woman frowned at Lily. "If a bolt were to strike the gondola, I would not want to be anywhere near that window." She got up from her seat and departed, followed by her companion.

"What's wrong with her?" Lily remarked. "I told her it was safe. And does she think that the electricity can get through the metal shell of the gondola? That's just silly!"

"You're correct, Lily," I said. "But you must also remember to be respectful of your elders."

"I'm sorry, Miss Ione." she said.

There was a murmur of voices from the other people in the lounge. Three couples got up from their seats and left. Four men at a table playing cards glanced at the storm but continued their game.

"Perhaps we should go as well," I said. "Although I love to watch lightning; it is such an astonishing display of nature's beauty. Rarely do people get the chance to see it from such a high vantage point."

"Why should we go, if it's not dangerous?"

"It isn't, not at the moment, but the storm seems to be moving quickly," I said. "Alright, let's watch just a little longer, and if the sailing becomes too rough, we'll head for our quarters."

"Okay," Lily nodded. The word was one of the many Americanisms she had picked up in New York. She still spoke with the British accent she had acquired in London, but it was not nearly as pronounced as when we had first met.

We watched in fascination as the clouds grew darker and closer. After the craft pivoted eastward, the roiling black mass was now off to the starboard side. Now and again a jagged stroke of lightning cast wild shadows in the dimly-lit lounge. Even the card players stopped to gaze out and comment on the storm.

Then the floor began to vibrate, and Lily cried out in surprise. "Miss Ione!"

"Quickly, to the wall, and hold onto the railing." We knelt down on the floor, gathering our long skirts around us.

"I left my purse!" Lily cried. "And your hat!"

"They'll be fine," I said.

The card players jumped from their seats and joined us by the wall, but not without grabbing their drinks first. The craft heaved and shuddered. The tables and chairs with their magnetized feet stayed upright but all the teacups, saucers, playing cards, and poker chips spilled out onto the floor.

"The captain said they'd avoid the storm," Lily said.

"I'm certain they're doing their best," I said. There was nothing we could do but stay as calm as possible and wait for it to pass.

The gondola heaved and swayed, causing my stomach to seemingly drop out from under me. One of the men, thankfully the furthest from us, became ill.

"Lord help us!" one of the men shouted.

Lily's complexion had turned white as the foam on the sea below us. I rummaged through my purse and found a small metal box, which I held out to her. "Here are some peppermints for your stomach."

"I'm okay, Miss Ione," she said.

As she spoke those words, the airship ceased its shaking. The storm was now receding in the distance.

"We're saved!" cried the man sitting next to me. "Thank God!"

"Amen," I echoed. "Come, Lily, let's go to our quarters. I'm sure the stewards will be here shortly to clean up." We fetched our belongings and exited the lounge.

"Not a moment too soon," one of the men was saying. "That lady and the girl were about to become hysterical."

As we walked through the corridor, still a bit unsteady, we heard the Captain's voice once again. "Our sincerest apologies, ladies and gentlemen, for the bumpy ride. It should be smooth flying from here on out. Unfortunately, we appear to have suffered a tear or two in the gasbag – nothing dangerous, but we will need to make an unscheduled landing for repairs. We are only a few hours north of the island of Crete, so we will be landing there."

"Oh drat!" cried Lily as we entered our tiny stateroom. "I was so looking forward to seeing the pyramids and the Sphinx and all the spooky mummies." She climbed onto the upper bunk bed and gazed out the porthole.

"Where's your sense of adventure?" I laughed. "I hear Crete is a beautiful place with interesting people and fascinating ruins. I for one am looking forward to it."

"It will be fun, I guess," Lily said.

I opened my trunk and began rummaging through it, trying to decide what dress to wear. Normally I preferred trousers for exploration, but my mother had bought us several lovely matching dresses which would be fun to wear for our arrival. I am a brunette of slight build, and if not for our differing facial features, people might be inclined to view Lily and me as sisters.

"I don't know what to wear," Lily said.

"Wear whatever you like. I expect it to be sunny, so bring your parasol."

"Not the parasol. I'll wear the new hat your Papa made for me, with the built-in compass and goggles. I want to bring my camera, and I shall need two hands for that."

It was a lovely summer morning as we disembarked at the airfield in the coastal city of Heraklion. After spending so much of my life in London, Paris, and New York, it seemed barely more than a village. When we emerged from the elevator I spoke to a steward and got the bad news.

"Sorry, miss," he said, "But there aren't a lot of resources for Zeppelin repair on Crete. The Captain says we'll likely be here for at least three days."

Lily looked downcast, so I squeezed her hand and gave her a smile. "Cheer up, we will have the opportunity for some impromptu sightseeing. I have read of recent archaeological discoveries here which have set the scientific world all abuzz."

There was one hotel in the town, practically empty until our cadre of fifty-plus Zeppelin passengers arrived. I felt sympathy for the poor girl behind the desk, who spoke no English and was forced to deal with so many impatient visitors.

"I thought we would be waiting in that queue forever," Lily said as we left the hotel.

"What a lovely place!" I remarked. "Sunshine, blue skies, cool sea breezes."

The town of Heraklion nestled on the hills rising from the shoreline. Its buildings were modest and weathered structures of tan masonry. Above the rooftops, we could see the dome of a church, and the slender minarets of a mosque a bit further up the slope.

"Where are the people?" Lily asked. "Do they take an afternoon siesta like the Spanish?"

"Perhaps they are indoors," I said. "Let's go get a closer look at the church. This kind of architecture fascinates me."

As I expected, the streets became wider and the opened up into a village square. Currently, it was as full of people as the rest of the town was deserted. There was such a crush of

251

spectators that it was impossible for us to see what the cause of the commotion was.

Above the hubbub, a man addressed the throng in a loud voice. He was speaking English, though with an exotic accent. Lily and I worked our way through the crowd until we could see.

The speaker was a tall wiry man with a two-day stubble and curly blond hair. He was dressed in a worn tweed suit and a cowboy hat with one side pinned up. Next to him stood a metallic humanoid, an automaton reminiscent of Angus, the cooking machine from the Epicurean Exhibition in London in the previous year. There was something familiar about the man as well.

The automaton was made of polished metal and resembled a knight's suit of armor, except that its head was that of a bull, with long pointed horns on both sides. Every now and then it would emit a puff of smoke or steam from its metallic mouth.

"Ah, I see we have some new arrivals. G' day ladies, step right up where you can see my demonstration. My name is Doctor Lancelot Forrest of the University of Melbourne and this rather intimidating chap is Farley, the steam-powered Minotaur."

"Brilliant!" cried Lily. She withdrew her camera from its case and stepped into the clearing, standing as still as possible while she photographed the amazing machine.

"He's an ugly one indeed!" called a man from the crowd, causing a few titters of laughter. I recognized him as a fellow airship passenger, a Prussian mechanical designer we had met in the observation lounge. "But what good is he? What useful function does it perform?"

"Besides being a doorstop or boat anchor?" someone else called out.

"Farley's function is secondary in importance to his origin. The design of this metal man is based on the ancient technology of Atlantis, which I personally translated using a codex found in a dig in the Nile Valley in the latter part of the previous century."

"Um, sir?" Lily said, as she put away her camera and addressed Forrest. "May I say something?"

"Certainly!" the man beamed. "I'm delighted to see a young person taking an interest."

"We learned in school that Atlantis is just a story, an allegory for Plato's ideal society."

"Smart girl!" Forrest exclaimed. "You were paying attention to your teacher. Tell me, lass, are you familiar with the works of Ignatius Donnelly?"

"No," she admitted.

It was then that I realized why the man had seemed familiar. I had heard the Doctor's name from my father, who had corresponded with him for a time.

"Ignatius Donnelly," I said to Lily, loudly enough for all to hear, "Wrote several books on the lost continent of Atlantis. He believed it was not fictional, but an actual place."

"Right you are, madam!" Forrest replied. "Atlantis," he addressed the crowd with dramatic, sweeping gestures, "Was a font of science and wisdom that perished around the time of the Great Flood that is chronicled in the Bible. It is my belief that Mr. Donnelly was wrong about the location of the lost world, and that it was not a continent, but a city, and that it was located not beyond the Mediterranean Sea but within it."

The crowd, who had been silent for the previous exchange, erupted into a hubbub of jeers and comments. "Humbug!" someone cried. "Madness!" said another.

"If I'm mad," Forrest cried, raising his voice, "How do you explain this? Farley, walk!"

The bull-headed machine shuddered to life and began to walk, raising one leg and then the other. The crowd fell silent and watched in rapt attention. I was amazed. The metal man Angus had moved on wheels; this was the first time I had seen a machine walk in the manner of a human being.

"It's astounding!" someone shouted. The children in the crowd shrieked in delight.

"How does it do that?" asked Lily, her eyes wide with surprise.

"I have no idea," I said. "But I think he's a genius."

"Farley, left!" Forrest commanded.

The automaton turned left and was now walking directly toward us. It emitted a huge puff of steam from its mouth, causing Lily to giggle.

"Farley, stop!"

The machine didn't stop. It didn't even slow down. The crowd parted around us; a little girl screamed as her father scooped her up. I grabbed Lily and pushed her to the side, causing both of us to tumble to the ground.

"Stop!" Forrest bellowed, running toward us.

At last the machine halted, in the very spot where we had stood a moment before.

"My apologies, ladies!" Forrest cried. "The noise of the crowd made it difficult for Farley to hear." He extended a hand to help me up off the ground.

Lily had already gotten to her feet and was fuming in anger as she brushed the dust off her skirt. "Your stupid machine has spoiled my new dress, and almost broke my camera!"

"Your machine is not safe," I said. "Lily could have been seriously injured."

"Only if she had stood there unmoving, which she did not, of course," Forrest said, smiling as if nothing untoward had happened.

"That thing is a menace," said an English woman I also recognized from the airship. "You should be reported to the authorities."

The crowd was now dispersing, people muttering and shaking their heads in disgust. I saw windows and doors opening in the shops and houses surrounding the square, as the townspeople peeked out at us. An olive-skinned man in a blue uniform emerged from one of them and hurried in our direction.

"Doctor, I warned you last time!" he cried in heavily accented English. "You have no permission to demonstrate machine. If you are not out of town by sundown I will seize machine and throw you in jail!"

"Yes, sir," Forrest bowed. "My apologies, sir. We'll be leaving now. Farley, follow!" He walked down the street towards the harbor, the machine clumping along beside him.

"Doctor," I called, hurrying to match their pace. "May I have a word with you?"

"Miss Ione!" Lily scolded.

I put a finger to my mouth to shush her. She gave a sigh of disgust and followed along.

"Doctor," I began, "Do you know a man named John Dfrdwy?"

"Dfrdwy? Why yes! I corresponded with him on design matters concerning miniaturized steam engines, such as the one that drives Farley here. Why do you ask?"

"I am his daughter, Professor Ione Dfrdwy of Brooklyn, New York. And this is my ward, Lily Chen."

"I'm honored to meet the both of you," he said. "Without your father's help, I wouldn't have been able to bring Farley to life."

"I thought you said the design was from Atlantis," Lily said.

"It is, Lily," Forrest replied. "All but the motive power, which was some mysterious source I could not discern. It is a technology that at present is still lost to mankind."

"Doctor," I said. "If I may ask, what is your purpose here? "

"I came here for the amazing new archaeological discovery at Knossos, the site of the palace of the legendary King Minos. As I believe that Atlantis was actually a great city on this island which fell into the sea, I expect I will find more Atlantean documents there."

"Then what are you doing here, and not at the archaeological site of Knossos?" I asked. I had recently read of the discovery, which was indeed significant and located close to Heraklion.

"Then you know Sir Arthur Evans, who is managing the dig?" he said. "As he did not accept my credentials, I was forced to take a menial job. In an effort to get in his good graces, I offered Farley's services to assist in the excavation. Alas, due to a vile prank by Evans' students, Farley demolished the canteen cart where the food was prepared. We were banished from the site."

"And then what happened?" Lily asked, a bit short of breath from keeping up.

"I have been trying to raise funds to continue my research. Unfortunately, the townspeople will not assist me. They are a superstitious lot. The local priest declared that Farley was a demon, which is why the villagers hide in their homes when we are about. I was about to give up when I heard that the Maria Theresa was landing here. I saw an opportunity to request help from educated folk such as you."

"By showing them the automaton?" asked Lily.

"As proof of the value of my research," replied Forrest. "If the ancient texts allowed me to make a functioning mechanical man, who knows what other wonders I may discover?"

"Sadly, I cannot assist you," I said.

"Professor, am not asking for your money. It's just that I'm pleased to meet someone with an open mind. Unfortunately, I find myself in a dilemma – I need to find a new place to stay, outside of Heraklion, one that will allow me to keep Farley." He glanced at the machine which trudged along beside us.

"Perhaps you--" My reply was interrupted by the loud roar of a gasoline engine as a motorcar zoomed up beside us. I grabbed Lily's hand and pulled her out of the street onto the front step of a nearby house. The vehicle screeched to a halt next to the Doctor, throwing up clouds of dust from the dirt street. The back door flew open and two burly men sprang out. They wore the robes in the manner of the Near East, with thick beards and red fezzes upon their heads. Speaking harshly in a language I didn't recognize, they grabbed Forrest and shoved him into the vehicle.

"Great Jehoshaphat! Who are you people? Release me at once!" The men ignored his protests as they piled in beside them. The vehicle sped away, leaving us in the dust. The steam-powered minotaur continued down the street without pause. "Farley, stop!" I cried. It halted, its steam engine purring softly as it stood and waited for its next instruction.

Also from Nakota Publishing:

Centrifugal Force by Vaughn Treude

In this novel of a probable near future, America is sliding ever further towards tyranny. Dissident blogger Joel Walter is wanted for a crime he didn't commit. His computer-hacker friend Nephi introduces him to an underworld where technology is Americans' last bastion of freedom and privacy. Despite pervasive surveillance, Joel decides to assume a new identity and disappear into the technological underground. Ever-increasing repression drives Joel, Nephi, and others into open rebellion in a desperate bid to retain their precious liberties.

Fidelio's Automata by Vaughn Treude

A stolen invention threatens his dreams. Fidelio Espinoza, a brilliant and idealistic young Cuban, arrives in early 1900's America with the goal of perfecting his automaton, a machine that will free humans from the dangerous, backbreaking work of mines and factories. Here he meets Hank, a cowboy turned Quaker who has vowed to atone for his sinful past. After a prototype of Fidelio's creation falls into the wrong hands, the two men join forces with Nikola Tesla to prevent this creation from being used in the service of oppression.

Works by Vaughn Treude & Arlys Holloway

Miss Ione D. and the Mayan Marvel

Strap on Your Goggles for Steampunk Adventure in the Jungles of Guatemala!

Introducing Miss Ione D: She's smart, she's tough, and she can cook! In her debut young adult novella, "Miss Ione D and the Mayan Marvel," 19-year-old Ione explores the ancient Mayan city of Tikal, where she makes an amazing discovery and faces unexpected dangers.

Short works by Vaughn Treude, available on Amazon:

"Found Pet" – a down-on-his-luck salesman adopts a strange furry animal that has a mysterious effect on the people around him.

"Fidelio's Dilemma" – young Fidelio Espinoza must decide whether to accept the respectable job arranged by his father, or to follow his dream of becoming an inventor.

"Love at Stake" – A lonely vampire tries online dating and meets his perfect match. But is she too good to be true?

Stories by Treude appear in the following Flash fiction collections by George Donnelly, available on Amazon.com:

"Ghost Writer" in *Valiant, He Endured: 17 Sci-Fi Myths of Insolent Grit*

"Happy Diversidays" in *Christmas in Love: A Flash Fiction Anthology*

www.ingramcontent.com/pod-product-compliance
Lightning Source LLC
Chambersburg PA
CBHW071137170626
46809CB00002B/664